Losers

Matthue Roth

PUSH

SCHOLASTIC INC.

NEW YORK TORONTO LONDON AUCKLAND SYDNEY
MEXICO CITY NEW DELHI HONG KONG BUENOS AIRES

GO THERE.

OTHER TITLES AVAILABLE FROM **PUSH**

Kendra	*Splintering*
COE BOOTH	EIREANN CORRIGAN
Tyrell	*You Remind Me of You*
COE BOOTH	EIREANN CORRIGAN
Being	*Johnny Hazzard*
KEVIN BROOKS	EDDIE DE OLIVEIRA
Candy	*Lucky*
KEVIN BROOKS	EDDIE DE OLIVEIRA
Kissing the Rain	*Hail Caesar*
KEVIN BROOKS	THU-HUONG HA
Lucas	*Born Confused*
KEVIN BROOKS	TANUJA DESAI HIDIER
Martyn Pig	*Dirty Liar*
KEVIN BROOKS	BRIAN JAMES
The Road of the Dead	*Perfect World*
KEVIN BROOKS	BRIAN JAMES
Ordinary Ghosts	*Pure Sunshine*
EIREANN CORRIGAN	BRIAN JAMES

ISBN-13: 978-0-545-06893-2
ISBN-10: 0-545-06893-2

bs"d

12 11 10 9 8 7 6 5 4 3 2 1   8 9 10 11 12/0

Printed in the U.S.A.   40
First printing, October 2008

"I don't want to be a loser. I want people to like me."
"But you hate everyone."
"Yeah, but I don't want them to hate *me*."

—Gwen Stacy, *Ultimate Spider-Man* #40

1. SPEAK MY LANGUAGE

I lost my accent over a long weekend in ninth grade.

It started on a gray Thursday in September, the first day of school. All morning, I'd been feeling like a total alien. My passport might say NATURALIZED and my accent might sound Russian, but I'm not talking foreigner status here — to everyone at North Shore High, I was a genuine, bona fide alien, three eyes and eight tentacles. While everyone else was giving each other once-overs, offering up shy smiles at prospective friends and potential crushes, people were shooting me baffled looks, as though I'd landed from the planet Koozbob instead of just Russia.

It wasn't like I was fresh off the boat, either — like I couldn't speak English or I was still dressed in geeky Russian sweatpants or something. I'd lived in this country since I was seven. But while most of these kids had known each other for years, through the downtown prep schools and science clubs that normal smart kids attended growing up, I'd gotten into North Shore by dumb luck. Everyone else had been together for eight years — the same schools, the same teachers, the same cliques — and I was the newbie, trespassing on the natural order of things.

Witness this: My head slammed against the locker door.

The fist that was currently attached to my head, its nails digging into my hair, turned ninety degrees to the right. My head turned along with it. I gave a short moan, more from instinct than protest. The locker's air grates dug into my eye, and I squelched it shut, just as a precautionary measure.

Jupiter Glazer, I told myself, *you have got to find a better way to make new school friends.*

"Like I said," my attacker said, blubbery and full of spit and bile. "You went and got real lucky. This new locker of yours is prime real estate. So I guess *your* locker is *our* locker now, right?"

Somewhere behind him, a crony of his belched up a laugh.

I decided that the path of least resistance would be to simply agree. Although my shoulder blades were currently at angles which I didn't think were possible, I did my best attempt to shrug them.

"Okay," I chirped as amicably as I could muster.

I just need to tell you: I was not new to this.

I was new to this school, this neighborhood, this life. But I'd been getting tossed around since I was a baby. I was born in Zvrackova, a city so small even its own suburbs had never heard of it. And then, on my seventh birthday, I flew to America. My parents told me it was a birthday present. I didn't entirely believe them — fleeing our home country under the cover of night, cramming all our earthly possessions into a couple of suitcases, it wasn't the kind of surprise party that most kids my age got. But when my parents called me into their bedroom that night and told me to pack everything, that's what they called it. A surprise party. I'd never even had a non-surprise party before.

I was flown all the way from Russia to Newark International Airport with just a single change of underwear. For other people, America was where you could practice religion freely, start a million-dollar enterprise, or buy as many cartons of cigarettes as you wanted. For my parents, it mostly meant the freedom to work, not wait in lines all day. As my mom tells it, I was just as eager for the land of free and plenty as she was, where she could buy as many multi-packs of generic allergy medication and Kleenex as she needed.

When we finally landed in America, my parents became our new country's biggest fans. They bought CDs of the worst country music and the out-of-date '80s hard rock they were never allowed to listen to in Russia when they were younger, hair bands like Poison and RATT. They ate at McDonald's every chance they got. They watched TV like addicts, borrowing liberally from sitcom punch lines the way other people quoted Shakespeare. And they taught me to appreciate the gifts that America gave us — gifts like free business enterprise, voting for president, and going to public school.

There were other lessons I learned on my own in my fourteen years of life on this planet Earth, spanning two continents, ten thousand miles, and countless school bullies. For example, when two hundred pounds of man-flesh comes at you with an attitude and an agenda, it is the ideal moment to start adjusting your point of view.

Especially when that two hundred pounds was shrouded in a T-shirt formerly owned, according to its insignia, by a band called the Thrill Kill Kult, and the fists were garlanded by two (allowed in school, but only barely) bracelets studded with metal spikes. Add to this a (definitely, totally not allowed anywhere near school property) metal spike collar, and a goatee slicked with enough oil and hair gel to render it as sharp, pointy, and lethal as any knife he could have smuggled in.

So, yeah. In the moment, agreeing with him did not seem like a bad idea at all.

Bates was so surprised, he un-crunched his fingers from my head immediately. "What did you just say?" he demanded in a roar that sounded like a lion accidentally swallowing a small frog.

I chose that moment to enact my denouement.

I ducked beneath the arch framed by the bodies of Harris Bates — the owner of the fist — and his best friends-slash-sidekicks, Nail and Anarchia, the pillars of said arch. Between them, there was enough metal on their clothes and in their bodies to set off the school metal detectors two floors away.

I dived between their bodies and onto the floor, skidding an elbow on the linoleum. I slid to a stop, hopped up, and leaped straight into a run.

I made the mistake of turning back to see if I'd lost them. They were right behind me. They exchanged glances, which turned slowly into evil smiles. Then they started after me, foot darting over foot, one after the other.

My first steps were clumsy stumbles.

In seconds, they had turned into a full galloping run.

I shot down the basement corridor, feeling the sudden slap of recycled air against my face. My chin-length hair beat in my eyes, then flew back as I gained speed. The hall soared past in a blur of *You Can Do It* posters featuring cute animals and rock stars that hadn't been cool for at least seven years. I feinted to the left, then dived right, dodging the girls' soccer team, who had chosen that moment to congregate in the hall and talk about the championships, or the captain's date last weekend, or something else to do with scoring. Only one thing was on my mind: the need to *get out*.

Then I felt the tiny, sharp pull of an inhumanly small hand affixing itself to my collar.

I spun around, finding myself face-to-face with a girl in a soccer-team uniform. Her smile was like a daytime TV commercial. She talked too fast for me to get nervous. "Hey," she said. "Are you the guy that Bates is chasing?"

"What?" I glanced back over my shoulder. Bates and his compatriots were standing in the main doors of the hallway, looking left and right, hungry predators in the midst of a hunt. "Oh . . . yes. This would be me."

"Then get in here. We can hide you. He's an asshole."

With her hand still on the scruff of my collar, she threw me down and into the circle of soccer girls. I crouched low, my knees pressing against the linoleum floor. I looked up at my newfound friend, flashing her a quick smile of thanks. She scowled down at me and, the next thing I knew, I felt a sharp crack on the back of my head.

After that, I didn't pick up my head for a while.

For a second — just a second, I swear — I'd caught a glimpse

5

below her skirt. She was wearing standard white underwear, slight traces of a lace pattern on the edge where it met her thigh — nothing like what I had imagined girls' underwear to be like.

But — on the other hand — I had actually seen panties.

Guilt began welling up in my head. I wondered if she was feeling violated. I wondered if she knew it was an accident.

And then I realized: Right now, I was surrounded by girls in miniskirts. And their legs were all at the level of my eyes. It was like some bizarre dream that's about sex but isn't sexy at all. A solid, unbreakable fortress of girls' legs, every shade of the spectrum from post-summer tan to solid black, quivering and twittering in time with the uninterrupted giggles of gossip that came from above. "No *way,* really?" said one girl, and her legs crossed, hugging each other at the knees. I tried to listen harder, as if, now that I was a foreigner in jock girls' country, I should maybe learn the language.

But, no. After a minute or two had passed, my original savior yanked me up. "They're gone," she whispered.

As I stood, still glancing around to calm my red-alert nerves, the constant conversation seemed to fizzle out. The girls started looking at me. It seemed like, for the first time, everyone else had noticed that they were acting as my firewall. And they did not look happy to be doing it. The bell rang and, like a ring of dancers in a Broadway show, the circle dispersed, each girl prancing off in a different direction to her respective class.

God. I hadn't even opened up my mouth.

I hadn't even *met* them. They'd barely seen my face long enough to decide whether I was ugly or not. How did they already know to write me off as a nerd? What is the invisible secret mark that makes popular kids intrinsically recognize their equals, and makes them rope off the rest of us into the dim and dreary purgatory of normality?

The rest of the day didn't go much better. My Bio teacher thought that Jupiter was a girl's name, my Spanish teacher tried to pronounce my name in Spanish, and my history teacher couldn't find my name at all, and insisted that I wasn't actually registered to go to school at North Shore. Just as she was about to send me to the principal's office for rerouting or deportation or something even more sinister, I told her to let *me* have a look at the roll, grabbed it out of her hand, and found myself listed under *J* for *Jupiter, Glazer* instead of *Glazer, Jupiter.* I guess I said it a little more aggressively than I absolutely needed to. From behind me — and I was standing right in front of the classroom, at the teacher's desk — I heard someone go "*daaaamn,*" followed by a low whistle. A murmur spread among my fellow students.

The corners of my teacher's mouth twitched. From the back of the room, Devin Murray and Vanessa Greyscole and all the not-ready-for-prime-time sorority girls made sounds like stuck noses, just aching to laugh out loud at me.

After school, totally deflated, I wrestled with my new role of being the most well-known kid in school — for all the wrong reasons. Between Bates, the teachers, and my own social awkwardness, I had made my reputation for the next four years. If I went home now, that would just be like admitting total defeat. Instead, I moped around the hallways, watching the population dwindle to a few stray students. Finally, I found the computer corridor.

A good fifteen minutes after the last bell rang, Vadim V. Khazarimovsky, my only friend in the world, ambled out from the Mac lab. He opened his mouth, the familiar Russian syllables flowed out, and it felt like the non-brain-damaging equivalent of snorting crack straight into my brain. Just hearing Russian, the language that I'd grown up with, the language that actually sounded like a language instead of a movie soundtrack, set me at ease. It was like the Saran Wrap that had been wrapped over my mouth all day had just been peeled away, and I could finally, actually breathe.

"How did you know where to find me?" he said in Russian, blushing a little. Whenever we were together, we slid back into Russian.

"How long have we known each other?"

"Point taken. Jupiter, this school is the mark of utter insanity. Advanced coursework, my ass. I can't even tell you how *basic* the work in —"

"Hey, Vadim. Not to interrupt your own sob story, but I almost got pummeled into submission third period by this guy the size of Long Island."

"Yes, I know. But have you been to —"

"You *know*?"

"Yes, this news was all over school. In my social studies class, everyone was like, 'Are you related to that other Russian kid, the one Bates pummeled?' Jupiter — *comrade* — you need to watch out for yourself. My reputation can't take much more of this before I become a prime target."

"Excuse me? Vadim, have you noticed, I'm *already* a prime target?"

He gulped. He looked around nervously, to his right, then his left, and took two giant steps backward.

"Look," Vadim said, glancing at his watch, "sorry, man, but I have to go to this meeting with Mayhew. He wants to talk to me about possibly skipping me out of Decanometry."

"Mayhew?"

"Yeah, you know who —"

"*Doctor* Mayhew, you mean? The current principal emeritus of our school? You have a *meeting* with him?"

"Yeah. Anyway, my Deco teacher was talking to him, and he thinks experimental maths might be holding me back from —"

"Decanometry."

"Yeah. It was in last month's issue of *SciAm*. It's similar to Trig, only polydimensional. Anyway, you should catch up with me later. Come over after school?"

My eyes bulged, trying to keep up with him. *SciAm*, I knew from hanging out with him too much, was *Scientific American* magazine. Decanometry, I could only guess. I slid all that to the back of my brain.

"I will if I survive," I promised.

"Don't worry, Jupe. Just relax. Keep a low profile, and Bates will forget about you completely. He wouldn't want to run you down before Freshman Day, anyway."

"What in the hell is Freshman — oh, damn, Vadim. I really have to go," I said, patting his shoulder and moving him aside in the same motion. I'd just caught a glimpse of human flesh, heavy-metal hair, and black T-shirt, turning the corridor in the dwindling after-hours crowd. "Catch you soon."

"Come over later!" Vadim called down the steps at me.

"Can't!" I called back, already a set and a half of stairwells below him. I could only imagine what anyone overhearing would think of the loud Russian words cutting through their American air. "My parents want to take me out for dinner."

"After your first day of school? Why would they do a thing like that — as a consolation prize?" Vadim's heavy voice was amplified and accentuated by its echo in the stairwell, but I didn't answer him.

I just kept running.

2. THE WAITRESS

That night, to celebrate my allegedly victorious first day of school, my parents took me to the same place we went to celebrate virtually every family birthday, anniversary, and good report card ever — the Country Club Diner. In honor of the occasion, I wore a dress shirt with a collar. I had to try on all three collared shirts in my closet before I found one to mask the bruises that Bates put on me in the afternoon, but finally I looked presentable enough.

The Country Club was the most revered and upscale of all the dirty, deep-fried, oil-hanging-in-the-air and waitresses-who-call-you-"hon" places you can imagine. They even had a dress code there. It ran along the lines of "No Shirt, No Service," but it was still a dress code.

We waited in the lobby, which smelled of cheap, powdery mints and cigarettes, but not unpleasantly. I hated cigarettes with a passion — at my old school, my sixth-grade best friend Garfinkel told me I wasn't cool enough and stopped talking to me on the same day that he started smoking cigarettes — but

I really, really liked the smell of cigarette-inflicted lobbies. Maybe it just felt poetic. Maybe it was dirtiness and nostalgia all lumped together, although I wasn't entirely certain what it was nostalgia for.

Most of the waitresses at the Country Club Diner were totally creepy old ladies with hunchbacks and fake hair that stood straight up in messily asymmetrical beehives. Their skin smelled of Lysol and fish.

This time, though, we won the lottery. The waitress who met us at our table must have been the youngest there by about sixty-five years.

I tried not to stare.

She looked to be most of the way through high school, three or four years older than me. High cheekbones, longish blond hair bound up in a knot at the back, a small nose that turned up at the end. Her eyes were distant and vacant, like she'd been watching TV for hours, or maybe just working at a job that she longed to be rescued from. Right then and there, I felt a sudden injection of a fantasy whereupon I grabbed her hand, she ripped off the clip-on maroon bowtie and yanked the matching vest right over her head, and we ran out through the kitchen, took the first bus out of the Yards, and spent all night downtown, watching independent movies and drinking Italian espresso-based drinks that no one in the Yards had a hope of pronouncing correctly.

This fantasy tumbled apart the minute she opened her mouth.

"Ya want drinks now or just warter ta start wit?" she said.

Her voice was pure Yards, words running into each other like caramel, totally unmodulated. She sounded like every Yards girl did, a cross between a '50s B-movie gangster and a robot. When she stopped talking, her mouth kept moving, and her rear teeth cracked a stick of gum so emphatically that my father winced in his seat.

My mother, otherwise known as the most neurotic person on either side of the Atlantic, was already scrubbing soup stains off the laminated menu pages with her napkin. "Can you tell me, which specials are for tonight?" she asked, her not-used-to-English voice making static bumps out of the language I'd worked so hard to get smooth. I sank a little lower in my chair.

"They're on tha firs page," said our waitress, hovering rigidly in front of our table, pen and ordering pad poised in the air.

I wondered if she was just putting on the accent as a front — maybe she, too, had learned to blend in with the crowds. I wondered whether, if we found ourselves alone together, she would whisper in my ear like a late-night anchor on the TV news.

Totally on instinct, I looked over at her chest. She was wearing a bleached cardboard name tag, also laminated. Beside the Country Club Diner logo, it said, in all capital letters, MARGIE.

My mother folded the menu shut, as if to demonstrate a remarkable feat of instant memorization. "I will have the tuna salad grinder," she announced to MARGIE, whose facial expression was growing more bored by the minute.

Without waiting for me or my father to order, MARGIE snapped her pad shut. "I'll be raight out wit your warters," she told us. "Youse can order then if ya want."

For some reason, I really wanted a Coke. Someone at the next table over had ordered one, and the way the ice cracked in the glass, the way the bubbles fought each other sizzling to the top, looked really appetizing. But there was this unspoken rule in our family: We only drank water at a restaurant. Partly this was because they always charged as much for a glass in restaurants as stores did for a two-liter bottle, and we were offended by that. The other half of it — at least, for my part — was that my parents had just invested all their money into the factory, the block-long warehouse inside which we now lived. Going out to a restaurant like this — sitting at a table that didn't used to be a conveyor belt, drinking out of glasses that weren't stained with factory dust — was a luxury to us.

I watched my father sip his water, taking great care to avoid brushing the ice cubes with his mustache. My mother was spending an inordinate amount of time adjusting the napkin (cloth!) to drape perfectly on her lap. I picked up my own glass of water, ran the tips of my fingers over the raised bumps of the meniscus, and realized that MARGIE was staring at me, waiting.

"Sir?"

Her voice was absolutely flat. I couldn't tell if she was making fun of me or not.

"Uh," I fumbled. My menu was open to the page of steaks. The words swam over my eyes, each sounding more barbaric than the last: sirloin, pink, rib eye.

"Omelet," I said, taking a sudden urge and running with it. "Spinach, tomatoes, and cheddar cheese, with hash browns, grilled hot and hard, extra paprika, and rye toast."

Her pencil scribbled fast to keep up with my order. When at last she had finished, she glanced up from her pad and flashed me a single, lasting, cold stare, the kind that pretty girls with long blond hair are wont to direct at miscreant boys such as myself.

"An omelet?" said my mother. "With eggs? This is what you get for dinner at a restaurant? I could make you omelet at home, for nothing."

"Is fine," my father was already starting to defend me to her. He grabbed my wrist, shaking it like I'd just won an Olympic trophy. "Tonight is his honor dinner. Jupiter can make his own choice of anything he want."

The waitress tapped her pen impatiently on the pad. She was smirking at me, as if to say, *You're fourteen years old and you still go out to dinner with your parents?*

I looked around at the rest of the restaurant. Old people in khaki shorts and sandals. A family with several children gathered at a round table in the center of the room, the parents impossibly young. They were both huge — fat, yes, but also *huge*, squeezed into their skin. Their haircuts and clothes were hopelessly Yards, either out-of-date or stuck in a timeless Kmart vortex. The husband and wife looked almost the same, dressed in their sloppy T-shirts, with four or five kids that were identical, or almost identical, arranged neatly in their own seats around their mountainous parents. They didn't look more than a few years older than me, that couple — *that* was the scary part. I wondered if that was going to be my future, a potbelly and a family of indistinct-looking kids straight out of high school.

There was another family in the restaurant that was clearly

15

Russian. You could tell. The parents didn't look American at all, and the kids looked way *too* American. Cheap button-down shirts and single-sheet pattern dresses for the adults, backward caps, sports-team jackets, and skanky skirts for the girls. Lots of visible electronics. Cell phones clipped to their belts, pagers in abundance, and, for some reason, sunglasses that they'd borrowed straight from the Junior Mafia.

All these families were clustered in a restaurant named after an American institution that none of us would ever have a shot at getting into.

The soccer-team girls were probably all out on dates with their boyfriends tonight. Even Bates was probably out with Anarchia or some other heavy-metal girl, doing God knows what in a dark basement somewhere. And I was going out with my parents after the first day of school.

I needed to get out.

"I'll be right back." Without really knowing where I was going, I stood up and shot off.

Going to the bathroom in a new place was one of my favorite things. I know it sounds gross, but bathrooms, when you're fourteen years old, are the only bona fide place where you can hide out from your parents. Everywhere I went with my parents, sooner or later, I needed to escape from them. And each place I hid out, each bathroom, was different. Some were sleazy, with cigarette butts all over the floor, leftover pee bubbling in the urinals. Others were clean, almost eerily hygienic. The best thing about bathrooms, really, was the graffiti. Everything from the trite-but-classic "Here I sit/brokenhearted/come to shit/ but only farted" to ruminations on the universe, to those almost-possibly-real girls' names and phone numbers written on the walls, either by vengeful ex-boyfriends or (please, God, please) by the girls themselves, curious to see what kind of teen-age boys were reading them.

I followed a hunch, and slipped into the hallway next to the kitchen. MARGIE was standing there, right in the doorway, staring at her nails. She looked utterly fascinated and utterly bored.

"Hey," I said.

She looked up from her nails. "Yeah?"

I took one hand out of my pocket, gave her a little wave.

"Whaddyawant?"

I counted the words in my head. *What. Do. You. Want.* Four words, and she'd managed to condense it into a single syllable. There had to be a Nobel Prize category for that.

"Uh, I was actually just looking for —" I said slowly, halfway into my sentence before I realized I was going to ask for the bathroom. *Bathroom.* There had to be a better word for it. Or, at the very least, a word you didn't have to use with girls. *Facilities? Lavatory?* In a flash, simplicity seemed like the coolest response, and before I could check myself I'd finished my sentence. "— the boys' room?"

Shit.

She didn't even blink. "Right over there," she said, nodding behind me.

I looked over my shoulder. There, on bright red plastic signs, were two silhouettes, the international symbols for *I need to go NOW.*

I blinked at her, briefly, coolly, as if to thank her without fur-ther sacrificing my dignity, and turned to follow her nod.

"Hey, wait." She tugged on my sleeve. I wasn't out of this yet.

"Yeah?" I spun around carefully, making sure she didn't let go of my shoulder.

"You look sorta farmiliar," she said. "Do ya go ta Yardley?"

Nathan Yardley High was just down the street. There were about three thousand kids there, bussed in from all over the Yards. Everyone from my old class went to Yardley — everyone, that is, except for the hydroponic nerds like me who placed into an accelerated high school on the other side of the city. I couldn't say yes, and I really, really didn't want to say no.

"No," I said, throwing all my cards into one basket. "I'm at North Shore. It's this special-admissions high school near town —"

"Wow," she said — still in that android monotone, but her eyes open in newfound appreciation. "Yeah, I heard of it. You must be pretty smart or somethin', huh?"

I shrugged. If I was now playing the part of a North Shore kid, I might as well do away with the false modesty. I was already feeling like roadkill, and I could use any brownie points I could get.

"Hey — I got to take my cigarette break now, or I don't get another one for another hour. You wanna come?" She nodded toward the door marked EXIT, which was right next to the door marked GENTLEMEN.

And then she threw me instead into the broom closet, shut the door behind her, inserted a single, long-nailed finger into the collar of her dress shirt, and yanked it down so that the shirt ripped in half, buttons flying everywhere, her lacy-bra'd breasts popping out like a cuckoo clock, like a pair of grenades, with me at ground zero. Her hair got in her face. Her hair got in my face.

Our tongues dived into each other like crazed monkeys battling, fingers grabbing each other, pulling into our flesh, trying to force our bodies even closer together. Her skin was white and smooth, like new, just-out-of-the-package soap. Her lips were thin and crisp. I tried to pull myself away, then relented, pressing my torso against hers, hoping against everything that she noticed, that she could smell how incredibly much I wanted her.

Oh my God. I am a teenage boy. I am loquaciously, disgustingly horny. I am horny for anything that moves. I have fantasies about the girls on the nine o'clock sitcoms, girls on the ten o'clock dramas, and the girls in the deodorant and car commercials in between. My head is in the gutter, and the rest of my body is squeezed right underneath it.

We stood right outside the exit door, a few steps away from the kitchen, and she pulled on the hoodie she'd brought out with her. It was tight. It pulled in her stomach and silhouetted her breasts a lot more clearly than the loose shirt and vest of her uniform. She drew a lighter and a pack of cigarettes out of the pocket and lit one up, barely looking at me as she drew the flame into her cigarette with a deep breath. Her hair bristled. It looked nice.

"So," she said. She looked at me expectantly, like my being here was a privilege, and now I had to earn it.

"So," I echoed, not sure what to say. I folded my hands in front of my belt, realized I was standing with the posture of a fifty-year-old college professor, and quickly slid them into my back pockets. "You live around here?"

"Yeah," she grunted. When she talked, the smoke curled out like a dragon's breath. "My parents got an apartment a few blocks away. I'm saving up so I can move out of that shithole and get my own place, probably another shithole. But at least it'll be my own shithole. You?"

"Yeah, kinda. Down where Yardley Ave stops being a hill and flattens out, over near the docks."

"Oh yeah?" she asked, taking a deep, impressed toke. "Rough neighborhood."

"Parts of it are. You learn to lay low."

"My boyfriend used to run DVD players for these guys, he was down there all the time. They kept them in one of those old warehouses, not even locked. You could just walk right in and help yourself. There ain't too many houses around there, right?"

I shrugged noncommittally, trying to cover up for the fact that I'd winced when she mentioned having a boyfriend. "There's a few. It seems rough, but it's mostly quiet."

"Man, that's not too bad. I bet I could rent a whole house around there for what an apartment would cost. That would be pretty tight. I could even have friends move in — of course, I wouldn't, that would kill the whole purpose of it. Hey, are there any houses around there up for rent now, do you know?"

"I dunno. I'm kind of, you know, taken care of."

"Still doing the parental thing, huh?"

She said "the parental thing" as if it was an extreme improbability that any child above the age of teething would ever live with his parents. Not sure how to reply to that, I played it cool. "They're not so bad," I said, offering up yet another indifferent shrug. "Mostly, we live in two different worlds. I think in English, and they think in Russian."

"Yeah, well, you don't *sound* like you think in English."

20

I could feel my face heating up. Now I was blushing furiously. I didn't say anything, not sure whether I should be offended or not. Other things about me that I was insecure about, I could hide. My accent stuck out like a bad hair day without a hat, like a zit that never went away. My hair was fuzzy and big, curls sprinting out in a Sideshow Bob 'do that required refreshingly little effort. She ruffled the top of it now, as if petting a puppy.

"Don't knock it," she said. "You're cute. And then you open your mouth and that voice comes out, that voice of yours, and it doesn't sound anything like you expect it to. I bet you're good at throwing people for a loop, yeah?"

"I'm alright," I said noncommittally.

"Nice. So, what's with the accent anyway?"

"What's with it? I'm with it, I guess."

"Heh," she laughed. She laughed in a way that sounded like she'd contemplated what she was laughing at, thought about it for a while, and she still didn't think it was funny. "If you were really swift, you'd say, 'What accent?'"

I didn't reply. Now I was listening to her voice, how much softer and less abrasive it had gotten while we'd been out here. "How about you, then?" I said. "Now you barely sound like you're from the Yards at all."

"Yeah, I dunno," she said. The gravel crept back in, but only slightly. Maybe because she was thinking about it now. "It's a defense mechanism, you know? You got to communicate with people on their level. You got to make sure they don't give you shit."

I waited.

For a moment, it seemed like she was in another world. Like there was something in her voice that she wasn't saying. Then she snapped out of it, and snapped back to looking at me. She laid a hand on my chest. I felt like I should leap back, like she'd just bumped into me — it was so direct and so forward and even, if only inside my brain, so sexual. Her nail was right over my nipple. Her palm was hot, and I wondered if she was going to pull me in to her and start kissing.

Instead, she let go. She stepped back like nothing had just happened.

"But, come on," she said, putting one hand on a hip, cocking a posture like she was examining me from afar again. "What's the deal with your accent? Are you an android, or is your larynx just on steroids?"

I gulped. "It's Russian. My parents are from Russia. We got airlifted out of the country when I was seven."

"Oh yeah? How was that for you?"

"I don't remember that much. My parents made me stuff all the clothes in my room inside a duffel bag in, like, ten minutes. They said to just bring the important clothes — they were too busy, they couldn't even help me — and when they unpacked they discovered I had only brought my holiday dress suit and a shitload of underwear. Oh, and *Where the Wild Things Are*, which was my favorite book at the time. Anyway, they hustled me out the door, to a plane, telling me we were going to a party. I stayed up the whole flight, gazing out the window, and fell asleep as soon as we landed. I woke up a few hours later, we were in this rusty recycled car, headed for the Yards, and then I turned into an American."

She barked out a bitter, dry laugh. "Damn, dude," she

said. "I think that's the first time I ever heard the Yards being a happy ending."

"Well, damn yourself," I said, trying to project some sauciness into my voice. "I didn't think I was up to the ending, yet."

She smiled.

For the first time, it seemed like I'd found something soft about her. Her voice, her chin, her eyes, even her breasts were so perfect, ample, and fleshed-out, plentiful in the way of Italian mothers and collagen patients, but perfect in the other sense of that word, too, stiff as a Renaissance picture. From her body, and from her attitude as well, she was the total opposite of me: totally composed, totally on top of her own social scene, and totally in control.

But, man, when she cracked her mouth open and let her smile poke through — awash in all her thin-lipped glory, crooked teeth swimming inside, gums the pale pink of someone who runs their toothbrush under the water instead of scrubbing their teeth at night — it was so imperfect and asymmetrical, so flawed and honest, that it actually made her look beautiful. I wanted to take that smile in my pocket and fall asleep with it under my pillow, to have it keep me warm through the cold of the warehouse night.

"And it isn't so happy, either," I said.

She opened her mouth and looked at me — *what do you mean?* — in the way that perfect people always do, those girls who say whatever they want and expect everyone else to love them for it. But then she closed her mouth, as if to take back that sentiment, and instead she reached over with those intense fingernails and pulled my collar down.

I winced again as she saw my battle scars. My knee throbbed, and its soreness wasn't visible but I imagined she could see my limp, too, even as I was standing still. She looked grossed out, as any normal person would be, but not revolted.

By which I mean, she didn't flinch. And she didn't look like she was going anywhere.

"Yeah, well, you know what?" she said. "It's gonna be."

I took a hard, long breath.

"After what we go through to get where we are," she said, "it better be happy. It fucking better be."

She brushed aside one permed curl from her forehead. I could see purple skin of her own beneath it, a nasty contusion that ran along most of her scalp.

And, at that moment, I was about to offer her a room in our warehouse. I was about to tell her, forget about my hormones, forget about getting an apartment of your own, I'll take you away from all this.

She reached down, ground the cigarette out with the heel of her shoe, and tossed the butt in the half-cranked-up window of someone's car.

I waited for her to say something, and then I realized that she was staring at me. Probably because I was staring at her legs, long and pale and enclosed in a showcase of nude-colored fishnets, still exposed in the air after the grinding of her cigarette.

She grinned at me and re-ruffled my hair. When she spoke again, it was like her accent had switched back on. Like everything that had just happened between us hadn't actually happened.

"Look, I gotta go back inside," she said. "Guess you do, too. Anyway, good luck and stuff. It was good talking with you, kid."

"Well, hey, thanks yourself," I said. "And hope to see you around, Margie."

"Margie? Oh, jeez, that's not me — I just forgot to bring my name tag. I'm only Margie for tonight."

I watched her climb the stairs, still in the parking lot, still stuck inside the memory of her legs. Her legs and her head. I watched as she hesitated for a moment on the precipice between the last step and the door inside, as if she was trying to decide whether she was going back in or not.

And then she did.

3. YARDS AND YARDS AWAY

Day Two.

Day Two was a Friday, which meant school was not quite as bad. Who was the School District genius who decided to start school in the middle of the week? You'd think they'd just wait till next Monday, so we wouldn't be *quite* so culture shocked twice in a row, but I didn't blame them. Friday in general had always been a chill-out day, a work-free day, and a Friday before you had any work to do in the first place was pure brilliance. I've learned not to look gift horses in the mouth.

I got to school in the nick of time, 8:14, a minute before the bell rang. After experiencing a momentary sense of disorientation, in which I suddenly became afraid that I'd forgotten where my classes were and everything else I'd learned on the first day, I spotted a fire alarm that I remembered running past yesterday. In a flash, everything came back, and before the minute hand could jump forward and toll its cruel fortune, I was sitting in homeroom, Advisory #405, sitting in the next-to-last seat in the class, right in front of Liz Gozner. I successfully managed to avoid Bates, and I successfully managed to avoid the embarrassing before-school time when everyone groups up, socializes with their friends, and checks out who the leftovers are, the ones without anyone to pair up with.

This was where I would sit, in complete and utter silence, until the bell rang.

This was how, in one form or another, every class that day progressed. When at last the final bell rang, I ran outside, feeling my lungs fill up and balloon for the first time that day. The North Lawn grass was wet and turfy below my feet. A cappella gospel songs that I didn't even know the words to were ringing in my head. Freedom had never felt so free.

So why isn't anyone else out here? I asked myself suddenly.

There was a thin trickle of kids leaking from the building — nowhere near the Friday afternoon exodus you'd picture. A few kids were milling about on the Lawn, throwing Frisbees, eating their lunch. *Lunch.* Oh no — slowly, sickeningly, like my blood had turned to a giant vat of oil, realization swam through my body. It wasn't the end of last period. It was the *beginning*.

I ran into class, ten minutes late, face-to-face with thirty gaping students. My classmates. They were supposed to be on my side, but at the moment, they were all giving me a single, unified dirty look, like we'd all simultaneously arrived in Hell and I'd accidentally stood against the button that turned off the air-conditioning.

Our teacher, Mr. Denisof, was scribbling away on the blackboard. Just then he finished the outline for the day's work, turned around, and found me standing in the front of the class. His mustache twitched, trying to make sense of the scene that I'd suddenly stumbled into.

"What's your name, young man?" he asked, in that soft voice, either incredibly insightful or incredibly patronizing, that teachers seem so good at.

"I'm sorry —" I managed to choke out.

He looked at me sideways through the narrow lenses of his designer glasses. "I *said*, what's your name?"

Before I could reply, a voice called out, "That's Jupiter Glazer." I didn't see who it was, and I was dumbfounded that anyone in the class knew my name at all.

Mr. Denisof was already over at his desk, looking down the roll book. "Glazer, huh?" he said. "What seems to be the problem, then, *Mister* Glazer?"

"I am trying to not make a problem — I'm trying for there to not *be* problem," I stammered, trying to explain. "I can't — I not —" My English was getting wavery, the way it always did when I got flustered. "I go sit now."

"Excuse me?"

"Please, I'm unable to — I'm not so eloquent —" My mouth moved quickly, in those foreign patterns of English words that I was suddenly totally unsure of how to pronounce. Did the *I* come before the *can't*? After? Was I not supposed to say *I* at all? I could feel myself second-guessing. From behind me, there came brief, scattered spouts of laughter, like a water fountain that was clogged by algae. I could feel myself reddening. I could feel my entire body starting to blush.

Mr. Denisof was standing behind his desk, scribbling something quickly on a tablet of pale green paper. He tore off the top sheet and handed it to me. "Here," he said, pronouncing each word slowly and deliberately. "I want you to go to the office. The principal's office. Do you know where that is?"

Mutely, I hung my head. I hefted my massive bag of textbooks onto my back, plucked the note from his fingers, and left the room.

The hall was totally empty, nobody lingering. By now, everyone was either in class or gone. There wasn't even an echo of students talking from the classes; it was still too early in the period for class participation.

Instinctively, the way every new student knows in their subconscious where to hang out and where to avoid, I found myself being drawn to the school office. The office was bustling, teachers standing around with coffee, office aides swarming the mailboxes, inserting copies of flyers for class announcements and start-of-year opportunities. The entire room seemed to gravitate toward a massive central desk with a brass nameplate that said MRS. LEPORE, no title. Behind the plaque was a self-important-looking woman. I handed the note to her without a word.

Equally without a word, she handed it back and nodded to a glass door across the hallway that said on it, simply, MAYHEW.

I left the office. There were three chairs next to Mayhew's door, looking both calm and sinister. Its ambiance was exactly what I remembered from the Russian airport: calm, stale, as if the very walls was saying to us, *You may think you're getting out, but we know the truth: No one ever goes anywhere.* Standard classroom chairs, plastic, with desks attached. The two closest to the door were empty.

Bates was in the third.

I took the seat that was farthest from him. I sat down quickly, without making eye contact, without looking up at all.

As if watching a movie, I could see myself sitting there, in third person, feet tucked under the chair, legs and shoulders pulled in tight. I was a pill bug, curling up to protect myself from danger, sheathing myself in the armor of my own skin.

The heat levels rose at least two degrees (ten, I corrected myself — home was Celsius, school was strictly Fahrenheit land). I could feel Bates train his gaze on me.

I heard plastic creaking. I heard the sound of a loud, sudden *snap*.

I looked over.

Bates had crossed his legs. Now he was cracking his knuckles, folding the fingers of his big, meaty paws together, resting them in his lap.

"So," he said casually, "what are ya in for?"

My breathing totally stopped. He wasn't brazen enough to jump me right outside the principal's office, was he? I contemplated my options: answer honestly (*no*), come up with something wiseass and witty and hope Bates wouldn't pound me (*no*), jump up and run as far as I could until someone caught me, either Bates or the assistant principal (*no*). I ran over the *no*s in my head, trying to judge which *no* was the biggest. I took a chance.

"DWA," I replied. "Driving while accented."

To my surprise, he neither remarked on the patheticness of not even having a decent, manly reason for getting sent here (possible examples: cutting class, a fight, snorting lines of coke in the bathroom), nor did he crack on my half-assed joke.

He just shrugged.

"What about you?" I remembered to ask, my politeness instinct snapping in.

Bates echoed his own shrug. "They're keeping me down 'cause of my religion."

For a second, I was sure he was going to tell me that he was caught sacrificing bunnies during lunch period and getting the blood all over the school toilets.

Then I spotted the enormous wooden rod lying across his lap. It was at least five feet long, curled at the top like the end of a violin, with swirls and globes and curlicues carved into it.

"They won't let me carry my staff," he said, by way of explanation. "In my old school, they used to let me — well, not *let* me, but nobody asked any questions. Here, they don't know what to make of it. I mean, it goes through the metal detector fine, but . . ."

His voice got choked up at the end, and there was a note of sadness in his words — real sadness, like the feeling I got in the back of my head and the pit of my stomach when I thought about the life I could be leading in Russia with friends who'd understand me and not think I spoke like I was retarded.

"Damn," I whispered, selecting my words as carefully as a surgeon about to slice. "That must suck."

Bates raised his hand up till it was right in front of his head, directly in his line of view. As if in slow motion, he curled his fingers until they were fist-shaped, capped his thumb over them, and cracked it. The crackle was resounding. His mouth and eyebrows clenched, face convulsed, and I could feel him heating up.

"Yeah," he said. "It so fuckin' makes me want to —"

"Jupiter?"

Bates quickly dug his still-clenched fist into his lap. His forehead unclenched, and his other hand took the bottom hem of his massive, oversized *Death Eats Everything* shirt and wrapped it over his fist to hide it.

I looked up. It was Ms. Fortinbras, who'd been subbing in my English class. As far as I could tell, she was a mellow, agreeable type, the kind of substitute teacher who doesn't make you listen to the lesson as long as you aren't out of your seat or texting with your phone above the desk.

"Jupiter, what are you doing here?" she asked, looking honestly puzzled. I'd been in the front row, and earlier today I surprised myself by actually paying attention to the lesson and even asking her a question.

"Mr. Denisof sent me to the principal's office."

"Yes, I can see that."

I gazed vacantly into my lap. "He couldn't understand my accent. He thought I can't speak English, and that I shouldn't come back to class until I learn the language."

"That's ridiculous; your English is absolutely fine. He's just a bigot looking for an excuse to whittle down his class size. Get out of here, take the rest of the period off, and if he still remembers on Monday that he kicked you out — which he won't — just tell him that your accent is from Cleveland or something."

"Tell him it's from Cleveland?"

"Whatever. If he asks, tell him he has to deal with me. But he won't."

"Um, okay." I nodded, unsure whether I was actually supposed to listen to her and get up out of my seat or just throw away the note and keep waiting.

Ms. Fortinbras jiggled the pile of papers she was holding.

"What are you doing sitting there? Get out of here! It's Friday afternoon. Go have a weekend or something."

I jumped out of my seat, straight toward the North Lawn, and clocked it out of there before Ms. Fortinbras could rethink her verdict or before Bates decided to kick my ass for getting out of my appointment when he was still in line for his own.

The bus to the Yards was full when I got on. Almost half the chairs were empty, but there was somebody sitting in at least every pair of seats. Philadelphia transit buses all have two rows of seats, with a few choice single seats on the left that get filled immediately. On the right side of the bus are pairs, two-by-two rows of seats. The people in those seats shot me hostile glances as I walked down the aisle, everyone trying to protect his or her territory. I slid in what I thought was the only unoccupied pair left, and hesitated halfway down, realizing that someone was sitting there, too short to be seen from in front. Then I realized that person was Vadim.

"Why are you leaving early?" I asked him, settling down into the barely comfortable seat lining, a scratchy felt.

"My Organic Chem teacher threw me out of class," Vadim replied.

"He threw you out?" I gasped, not comprehending. "For what? For knowing more than he does?"

Vadim looked at me with innocent, unsuspecting eyes. "Yeah," he said. "Actually, for that exact thing."

"Well, damn," I huffed. "It's official: This school has no sense of decency."

"Nah," he said. "It's cool. I think they're gonna skip me up a grade."

"Another one? But you've already skipped fifth and seventh . . ."

"What can I say?" Vadim made a Groucho Marx caught-in-the-act face. "They know talent when they see it."

"Yeah," I echoed blankly. I stared out the window and watched the houses go by.

The Yards, the neighborhood where we lived, was the dusky, dingy attic of Philadelphia, the horrible family secret that everyone wished could stay buried. Only, in the case of the Yards, the secret wasn't anything terrible or awful or lewd — it was just smelly and boring. In the '50s, the Yards were shipping yards, where all the city's commerce came from, and the neighborhood was full of eager, young immigrant families. But since then, the buildings stayed the same and the neighborhood degraded, to the point where not even immigrant families would live there — unless they had absolutely no savings, no self-respect, and basically no hope.

Ask me how I know.

As the scenery changed from houses to dilapidated shacks, we both grew uneasy, the way we always did when we took the bus home. I scratched at the ghost of an itch on the back of my neck. Vadim touch-typed with his fingers onto an imaginary keyboard on his knees.

"So," Vadim piped up, restless. "Want to come over?"

Want to come over? Hadn't this been our pattern for the past seven years? Since we've been in America — since we've been each other's only friend — nothing's changed but the verb. *Want to come over and play? Want to come over and chill? Want to come over and hang out?*

And all this summer, as soon as the factory let out for the day, more often than not I'd rip off my heat gloves, throw on a fresh T-shirt, and run over to Vadim's.

Oh, shit. The factory.

"Oh, shit," I said. "I can't. I promised my parents I'd try to keep helping out in the factory after school."

"Come on, Jupiter. Just because your social life revolves around your parents' pathetic excuse for an immigrant job doesn't mean the rest of the world should have to suffer with you."

I gave him a look, half ire and half fire. One of the cardinal rules of being friends with me was not joking about the factory.

Vadim knew that. But he also knew that sometimes I needed to be pushed over the edge. There was a glint in the little eyes behind those heavy frames that flashed insecurity, flashed fear, but also flashed a canny intelligence. "Jupiter, give me a *break*," he half said, half whined. "Give yourself a break. You go home every day and help on the assembly line. And you've said yourself, you're usually too worn out from school to make much of a difference. Sometimes the bus gets caught in rush hour and takes twice as long, and you might get there too late to be of any practical use anyway, so why force yourself to succumb when your estimation might not be of any quantitative value by the time you get there?"

I gaped at him, not sure how to argue against that — in fact, I wasn't really sure what his argument *was* to begin with. Still, Vadim was smarter and thought faster than I did. I always figured the U.S. government would come and take him away to a secret underground base for hyperintelligent kids one day. So, I decided, why not trust him on this one?

The bus screeched to a halt at Vadim's stop, still half a neighborhood away from my house. Vadim glanced back over his shoulder. I took a breath, wrapped my backpack strap around my hand, and hopped off after him.

As soon as Vadim and I were in private, we switched to Russian. That big, glazed-over curtain, which half blotted out the rest of the world when I was in public, fell away with the Americans and the bus stops and the rest of the world. This was the only place I really felt safe — and I didn't even with my parents, anymore, those people who loved this country so much they'd named me names from English magazines, who wanted everything it offered — the wealth, the language — so much that they tried to be normal. And, in trying, made me feel like even more of a three-legged space alien, so much that I had to run away to Vadim's to function.

Hanging out in Vadim's room was something of an enigma. Every time I came over, I wondered: *What exactly is it that we're doing?* Today was no exception. I took a running start, leaped, and landed on his bed, at the highest point on the pile of assorted blankets, comic books, junk food, and dirty laundry. It didn't especially bother me. I pulled a bottle of Jolt Cola, the ultracaffeinated nerd soda, from under a pile of socks and cracked it open. Vadim plunked himself down in front of his computer. His eyes got wider, lost focus, and his entire body started to sway in synch with the movement of his hand on the mouse. I pulled an issue of X-*Men* from underneath my butt and began to read.

"So," Vadim said, his eyes not deviating one millimeter off the monitor, "what do you think of North Shore? Do you really think we're gonna make it there?"

"Sounds like one of us is already making it," I said. I flipped back a few pages in the comic, studying the first page quizzically. "What the hell is up with White Queen? I thought she used to be a psychic."

"She is. But now her skin turns into diamond, too," Vadim replied. "Hey, do you know Devin Murray?"

"Devin?" I shot up. "She's — uh, she used to go to Malcolm X with us last year. She did that sexy dance last Christmas with the girls in Santa Claus miniskirts." What I *wasn't* saying was that she was also, hands-down, the hottest girl in our grade — both in the traditional babe sense and in the very real sense, too, the kind that, every time you look at her face, it seems like her eyes are even bigger and her cheeks are even smoother than you remember her. She had the kind of face that was both totally honest and totally unapproachable — and she had the reputation to go with it. The longest she had dated anyone was Reg Callowhill, who was both an all-city lacrosse player *and* went to private school. Eight months after their second-date breakup, the world was still talking about it. "Why do you ask?"

"'Cause she's got an online journal, and she just posted this announcement about a party tonight in the Yards."

"The Yards? No way, Vadim — it's gotta be a practical joke. Her family lives on the other side of the Northeast, in those luxury converted lofts. She'd never be seen in public around here, let alone . . ."

"I'm telling you, it's right here. I completely just found her secret online journal."

I glanced at the monitor. Sure enough, at the top it said *Devin's World of Secrets*, and the background colors were yellow and red, North Shore's official color scheme. Trust Devin to wave the patriotic flag fresh in the first week of school.

"'It's the social event of the season,'" Vadim read. As he went on, the words sounded like alien dialect coming from his mouth, popular-girl grammar with his thick Russian accent. "'Come one, come all, to the first annual North Shore Opening Week Stress-Free Zone! Mixers, pyrotechnics, and an iPod DJ station. Help the North Shore freshman class kick it in style, and get those party impulses out while we still can.'"

He had me convinced — at least, convinced enough to put down the comic and come spy on Devin's World of Secrets.

"How did you find this, Vadim?"

"My parents were saying I needed to get out more, so I Google Alerted the words 'North Shore,' 'freshman,' and 'party,' and this was the first thing that came up."

"And you're sure it's the same Devin, the same North Shore? Her last name's on it?"

"Well, no. And if you read the entry, it appears like she's taking great pains not to reveal her real identity. All her friends are mentioned by first names only. But if you click here, you can see her user profile — her home city is Philadelphia, and her email's devinm at whatever. Hey, isn't this right near the factory?" He had just hit the browser's back button, and now we were back on the invitation. His finger was extended toward the screen, aiming directly at the party's address. It was a few blocks from where I lived.

"How the hell is everybody going to get there?" I said, ignoring the larger and more logical question of how in the hell did North Shore kids know that the Yards even existed?

Vadim had an answer for that one, too. I should not have been surprised.

"Either the bus system is doubling its output overnight," he said, "or kids who live in more financially gifted neighborhoods are allowed to drive way before the legal minimum. Well — either that, or they all have absolute suckers for parents."

Vadim scrolled down.

"Yep, I was right." He cleared his throat and read, "'If u need a ride, give me a call. And please' — this part is in all caps — 'DO NOT MENTION ANYTHING ABOUT THIS TO MY PARENTS!!! They are OUT OF TOWN for the weekend!' I wonder why she's not having the party at her own house, then?"

"Don't be depraved," I said, swigging the bottle of warm Jolt. "She's probably saving that for her own private after-party. Or for her boyfriend of the moment. That's what popular people do."

"You think the rest of the school was meant to see this?" Vadim asked. He lowered his voice, although I bet he didn't even realize it. "Or do you think it was just meant for her friends?"

"Does it matter?" I finished the Jolt with one final, belch-inducing gulp. "I think we've seen enough to consider ourselves invited."

I got home that night at 7:00, almost a half hour after the factory closed. With thoughts of Devin's party still filling my head, I wrapped both my hands around the two-foot-tall door handle and swung open the single heavy door.

Or, at least, I tried to. It took me a minute of pulling and grunting before I realized it was locked. Padlocked. From the inside.

"Hold on," came my father's voice, sounding distant and distorted as it came through the sheet metal. "Is already locked up for night. I open."

"Why the hell did you lock the door, Dad?" I called through it.

"Your mother she does not want the door open so late. Also,

have been break-ins in the area lately. Also, we don't know what time you get home. Also —"

The door, with a massive nerve-rending squeal, slid open.

"I do not intend leaving open for the whole night long, waiting for you."

Without saying a word, he let go of the door, turned, and started to walk away, back toward the house area of the factory — the small alcove with partly upholstered sofas and a TV; the makeshift kitchen that had been makeshift for years, with plywood countertops marking its borders; the second-floor foreman's office, looking over the assembly line and the main room of the factory, which was converted into my parents' bedroom.

Yeah, this was where I lived.

Seven years ago, but I still remember it. The three of us sat in a gloomy, drab-looking room that looked like both the airport in Russia and the North Shore principal's office. We sat in a line: my father, me, my mother. I had never been on the same level with them, physically, before. Even at the doctor's office, one of them was always standing. And I had never before seen them looking as glum as they did now, facing a huge, monstrous desk, and a balding man whose glasses seemed to be larger than his head.

He was from the Jewish Federation. He was from the organization that, as far as I could understand, had brought us here. To America.

He spoke a lot. Occasionally, one of my parents would interrupt. I only gleaned a few words: *housing developments* and *integration into normal American neighborhoods* and *there's simply no room for more families.*

40

I kept thinking, *He keeps calling us the Moore family.*

At the very, very end, I remember him saying something to my father, and my father's voice brightening in response. It sounded like an offer. It sounded like he was offering us a deal.

It sounded like my father was taking it.

"It's about the house," the man was saying. "The new housing developments are still full, and we haven't been able to allocate enough additional funding to secure you a house of your own."

"But the condos . . .?"

"The condos are more expensive than the houses."

"Oh." The threat of being sent back to Mother Russia loomed large above our heads.

The director offered a conciliatory smile. "We have, however, located a housing facility that does hold a couple and a seven-year-old boy, as per your specifications. It's . . . well, it's good and bad."

"Good and bad?" My parents had learned quickly that, when you don't speak a language, the easiest way to reply was to repeat back the last thing you heard as a question.

"Let's get the big news out of the way first: it's a factory."

"A . . . factory?"

"That's right. The good news is, the Federation will be able to cover a large portion of your rental costs."

"A factory what makes stuff? Factory is . . . active?"

"That's right. But the good news is . . . well, the location made it easy to find you folks jobs."

I stepped over the track and struggled to pull the door shut. It was the front door to our house — and yet, unsurprisingly, it didn't seem at all like coming home.

"Dad," I said, "it's seven o'clock in the evening. The *sun* hasn't even set all the way. I was just over at Vadim's house. . . ."

He didn't turn around. "What you were not doing over there?"

"Dad, you've got the grammar all wrong. It's 'what *were* you doing over there.'"

"No, I am right. What you were *not* doing is helping us like is your job. We have deadline today we not make. And what is more, we trust you come and then you not come. Not even phone call. How I am suppose to trust you when —"

"I'm sorry, Dad. I just needed to let loose —"

"You just need to what? You just need to work. You need to help pay for going out to the Country Club, Jupiter Glazer!"

If we lived in a normal house, this would be the point where one of us walked out of the room, slammed the door, and possibly broke a doorknob or a window while doing it.

The fact was, though, our entire house was a big, ugly, mangy, turn-of-the-century, dust-infested, single-room factory.

At some point, it was one in a fleet of identical factories, all owned by the same huge corporation. At some point, that huge corporation decided — as would any sane person — to get the hell out of the Yards. And the factories got packed away, boarded up, auctioned off, and downsized.

And that's how we ended up here.

Fifteen years ago, the factory had functioned at full capacity, working 24/7 to supply the American public with new elevator parts. Chain hoists, counterweights, electric motors, and hydraulic controls — there were assembly lines for each one. Gradually, sections were abandoned as business dropped off. Now, we lived in the abandoned parts of the factory.

"It's not that bad," I remember my father telling my mother. "At least it comes with a job."

And so, with only the smallest amount of social awkwardness, they joined the twelve-person crew of the elevator factory.

My father, shaking his head, racketed up the stairs, two at a time, to the foreman's office. They more or less still used it as a foreman's office, only, because it was a workspace from nine to five and our house for all the leftover hours, my parents kind of used it as their office for when they needed to get away from me, too.

I checked out the day's damage.

To the left was the kitchen area, a big open space with a stove and dining table and the countertops that had been there as far back as I could remember. My mother was in there, slicing up beets for the night's dinner.

"Hey, Mom," I said. "I'm home from school."

As if she couldn't tell.

True to form, she didn't look up. My parents either had a psychic connection, or a really good sense of smell — whenever one of them was mad at me, the other could detect it in the air.

In my partitioned-off room, I checked my phone and found a new text message from Vadim waiting for me. *How was the damage?*

I typed back: *Nothing unexpected.* We were used to doing damage control for each other after one set of our parents went on a rampage.

After a second, my phone buzzed again. *Just saw 2 Lexuses heading yr way. U really going?*

I hadn't forgotten about my promises. My bragging.

Of course I was going.

As I scrambled to get dressed — which basically translated into throwing off one T-shirt and jumping into a new one — I made an instant checklist in my head.

Things that sucked about living in a warehouse:

Never being able to get away from work. How cold it got in wintertime. The fact that, every second I was there, it was an active, painful reminder that my family was dirt poor.

Things that made the warehouse dealable, if only barely:

How big it was. And how soundlessly I could sneak out.

4. A NIGHT LIKE THIS

Right across from my bedroom window was the rooftop of the next factory over. I could never get the window to close all the way, and even in the summer there were drafts that kept me up late at night. Where else in the universe got drafts in the summer? Only the Yards, I guess — only inside this little piece of heaven in the shape of an industrial warehouse. So I was meticulous about oiling my window twice a month (I borrowed some castor oil from the assembly line downstairs), and that night when I pushed the window, the hinges flipped open without a sound.

It was a four-foot drop to the roof next door. Fortunately, the walls hugged each other tight. Not more than six inches separated the two buildings. My feet touched down. From there, I used a ladder that went from the roof to the ground.

Once my feet touched pavement, I was running free.

The address from Devin Murray's Web site was a few blocks away. Mostly I used the back alleys. In a few, people were out, sitting on bridge chairs around a streetlight or a backyard light, playing cards or listening to beat-up boom boxes or just chilling out in wifebeater shirts and sandals. I almost stumbled over Mr. Diggory, the wino who sometimes slept out here, but realized I was about to step on a breathing stomach and jumped a foot to the left, knocking over his wine bottle. I stopped and reached into my pocket for change to replace it, but he started to chuckle. "Don't worry about it, kid," he told me, not unkindly, as he brushed off his pants. "You probably done me a favor, anyway."

That was one of the things I liked about the Yards: No matter how screwed up everyone was, we all still met each other's eye.

You could see the party from blocks away. My first indication of its existence was a bunch of lost-looking kids in club clothes glancing at a printed-out set of directions on a corner. On an opposing corner, some drug dealers that I went to middle school with last year were laughing at them. The air was cool, stiff like winter, as if signaling the approach of an oncoming cold. Tonight seemed especially foreboding — the beginning of school, the first weekend of a new social scene, all of this curious information about my new high school's online underground social calendar.

You know the difference between bad parties and good parties? At bad parties, the only people there are your friends; at good parties, everyone in the universe is there. And this party definitely, definitely had everyone. Devin Murray certainly knew how to network. The trance kids were spinning music, the AV nerds were projecting a light show on the wall, and the jocks were busy trying to lift a massive, sumo wrestler–size beer keg out of the back of one of their minivans. So far, the effort was being met with little luck. Not that it mattered. Sajit, the class's token gay stay-up-and-party prima donna, was tending bar, mixing lavishly colored drinks into elaborate martini glasses, serving them up and trying to lecture people on each drink's name and social relevancy. Right now, a bunch of the soccer-team girls were staring him down, looking disgusted while he tried to convince one of them to try a Flaming Orgasm. "Forget it," said one girl, finally. "I can't deal with that name — it sounds absolutely gross. Just make me a Sex on the Beach."

I breathed a sigh of relief. Sajit was the closest thing to a friend I had here. We grew up in the Yards together and, in elementary school, we used to get beat up together. We rarely actually hung out together, but common black eyes was the sort of bond you don't just take for granted.

"Jupiter, my dear friend," he said once he saw me, following up his words by wrapping an arm around me and taking me behind the bar. "How in the hell did you end up at a dump like this?"

"I *live* in a dump like this, Sajit," I said, looking around to see if anybody heard. "You've been over to my house, remember?"

"*Hone*y, do you think that tonight just *happened*?" Sajit asked. I knew he was exaggerating his Pollyanna 'tude for the night, but I think he was only doing it for the effect. "Tonight is a gift from heaven. You might live around the corner from here, but tonight, you get to pretend you have no idea where the hell you are." He pointed at my chest, then turned over his hand, cupped it, and blew into it like he was blowing pixie dust all over me.

"What do you mean?" I asked, knowing full well what Sajit

47

meant, but feeling the need to keep him talking, to hold on to my conversation partner and to keep pretending that I knew what was going on here.

"You could be from downtown, South Philly, East Falls, even. You could have borrowed your parents' car, or rented one of those limos outside. It's the first weekend of school. Nobody here even knows who you *are* — oh, Jupiter, don't look like that; nobody in this place is going to recognize you from that scene with Bates. It's too dark and mood-lit. And, even if they do, whose side do you think they'll be on? Forget about the *first* first impression you made. Right now is when you make your *real* first impression. You're already wearing the coolest clothes of anyone here."

"What, jeans and a black T-shirt?"

"What, do you not read *Vogue?*" Without waiting for an answer, Sajit took me by the shoulders, spun me around, and gave me a soft kick on the butt with his foot. "Now, stop talking to me and get out there and *mingle.*"

I was about to reply with a "yes, sir," or some other typically dorky comment, but Sajit, social butterfly that he was, had already sprinted over to the far side of the bar, and started lecturing some jocks on the seductive qualities of certain Belgian beers.

I left my leash of Sajit, entering the vague and scary no-man's-land of the party. Navigating a party alone could be the most amazing experience ever, or it could be the worst. There were so many people to see, and so many conversations going on, and the only way to really be a part of them all was to be a part of none of them. I stood back, letting all the conversation trails flow through my ears. I watched jocks flirting with jocks,

48

goths discussing deep and impressionable matters in dark corners, the punk-rock kids dancing to lame pop-rock ballads in front of the speakers, and the normal kids, the ones who either transcended labels or feared dropping into a category, walking around the cliques and amongst themselves, dropping in and out of conversations with a casual, nonthreatening, no-stick attitude.

Kids passed me by. Kids said "hi" — not a first-day-of-school "hi" where the teachers force you to smile at each other and play nice, but the noncommittal, how-ya-doin' "hi" that signifies that the two of you are on the same level.

In reply, I nodded. A cool, detached nod. A nod in time with the music, which I still did not like, but which was pleasantly bland, agreeable to my sensibilities, coating my nerves with a light, white-chocolate-flavored layer. I might not come out from this party with any friends, and I might not learn any deep life lessons, but, dammit, I was having a good time. Hell, I was discovering what it meant to have a good time, independent of my dorky friends, independent of my parents. And that might have been enough of a life lesson for me.

I felt a finger on my shoulder.

"Hey, you're kind of cute. Do I know you?"

I caught hold of the finger with all five of my own and I spun around, still clamped tight, tracing the visiting finger to its owner.

It wasn't that hard. Even if I hadn't been holding on to her finger at that moment, she would have been impossible to miss. Three layers of smart-looking pink — tank top, the fluorescent trace of a bra strap beneath it, and a studded pink leather jacket that looked like it was straight out of a movie, high shoulder flaps and wide '70s lapels — hugged her conventionally hour-glass form, both concealing and teasing in a way that made it impossible not to look at her. Bright blue eyes peered out from under impeccably tossed blond hair, alternately dirty and bright yellow streaks. A pink headband held it all together.

"I'm sorry?" I said quickly — one of the only English phrases I could always say perfectly quickly, guaranteed to be without a trace of an accent.

"I'm Devin Murray. This is my party. Who are you here with?"

I fought the natural impulse to say, *No one brought me — I live down the street and your American hip-hop music is drowning out my ability to sleep.* Instead I just smiled and nodded — the cool kid response.

"What? Can you not speak English?"

"What?" I said, caught off guard. "Oh, yeah, of course I can. I'm Jupiter."

Her momentary falter of a smile leaped back into full bloom. "Oh. Sorry. It must be the music — I mean, it needs to be loud, but only so we can complain about it, you know?"

"Of course," I agreed. "Wow, Devin. That actually sounds sort of profound."

"Yeah. I like to think I can manage profound, once in a while. So — uh — how did you get here?"

That question again. I'd managed to dodge it once, and I wasn't sure if my luck could hold out a second time. The possibilities leapt up in my mind like a Choose Your Own Adventure book — one of the sadistic ones where, at the end of every choice, you died.

I decided to go with the truth.

"My friend Vadim hacked onto your secret online diary," I said.

She looked at me like she was trying to decide whether or not I was lying. I think eventually she settled on lying, because in one hot moment, she burst out in a huge, quick balloon pop of a laugh. "No, seriously," she said. "Are you with Crash Goldberg and his posse? Because I think they're about to —"

At that moment, there was a massive, resounding explosion that flared in the far corner of the warehouse. An explosion that probably nobody else in this entire party would realize came from approximately five full-size barrels of raw castor oil, the kind used in powering T-3400 power generators and in greasing assembly-line conveyor belts to run smoother. Screams came out. It took me a second to recognize those screams as the girls' soccer team, that slightly annoyed but mostly flirty screaming that they did just to get attention.

The fire clouds were dying. People stood around, lightly applauding.

What was I doing here? Among the popular kids, among these fifteen-year-olds who dress up like thirty-year-olds trying to look barely legal? These were the popular kids. These were the kind of kids I'd gotten teased by in elementary school, then ignored by in middle school. I remembered being relieved when the ignoring started. Why was I now trying my hand at climbing that stupid social ladder? Why was I having to smile and endure those girls who made *girlish* synonymous with *helpless?* I tried to think about what MARGIE would say if she was here, and failed.

God, my realizations were really hitting tonight, weren't they? Bullseye after bullseye. Devin saw my look of exasperation, and she rolled her eyes. "I mean, it's *cool* that Crash and his posse are so into spectacle, but do those girls have to act so five-years-old every time they blow something up?"

At that moment, a guy in a bright orange federal prisoner's uniform and a Che Guevara cap, eyes as big and hungry as a wolf's, with a face that could only be described as crazy-looking, zoomed past. He threw his hands on my shoulders and pogo-jumped way over my head, his face a few inches from Devin's. He swung on my shoulders. "Hey, Devin, man," he said in a wild voice that befitted the rest of him. "Did you like the show?"

"Yeah, gorgeous, Crash. It was beautiful."

"Now *that* was real American-made pyrotechnics. Rita designed the detonators out of Radio Shack toaster ovens, and McNeff the crime dog hooked us up with some juicy transistors." He mopped a trickle of sweat — oil? — off his brow. He suddenly glanced down, right into my eyes, and gave an approving pat on my back. "Hey, dude. Are you enjoying the festivities?"

It had been so long since it was my turn to speak that I almost forgot to do it. "Oh, yeah, absolutely," I piped up at last. "It was awes — "

"By the way, thanks for inviting your friend," said Devin. "We're all *totally* into Jupiter. He's a few notches up from the usual hackers."

"Oh, um, definitely." Crash, still perched atop me, nodded approvingly.

"Are you gonna get some of your peons to clean that up? I have a three thousand dollar deposit on this place . . ."

"Already done, my good lady." He climbed off my shoulders, gave a salute, and scampered off.

Now that this Crash kid was gone, Devin turned her attention back to me.

"Heh heh." I gave a little nervous laugh. I was sure the game was up now.

"Yeah, I know. He's kind of a dork, isn't he? But it takes all types to make the world go round." She looked around the place like a monarch surveying her kingdom. Some of the soccer team girls were just now coming down from their spaz-outs, and a bunch of guys in sports-team jackets were calming them down, giving them neck rubs. "After all," she noted, "nothing sets off jock love like a nerd attack. And, by the way, you *utterly* aren't from around here. I've been listening for it in your voice."

Panic. Sheer, total panic.

"I don't know what you're talking about," I said.

"You think I'm crazy? Look, I'm from East Falls. Which is practically *the* capital for stuck-up, prissy princesses who are stereotypes of stereotypes of themselves. I grew up speaking half like a movie character and half like I was born in England. Then, in fifth grade, I started taking swimming lessons downtown. Olympic-size pool, taught by a former underwater stunt double from L.A. — all that impressive stuff. But the other kids there had all grown up downtown. They could spot my phoniness three lanes away. So I listened to the way I was speaking, and then I listened to the way *they* were speaking, and I just dropped it."

"You just dropped it? How?"

"Okay, let me try. Um. Did you hear how you said *dropped?* You swallow up the *o*, you roll the *r*, and you squish the *p* and *d* together at the end. Listen to the way I said it, just from what you remember."

"Dropped."

"Close. *Dropped.*"

"Dropped."

"Now try it slower." She said *dropped* again, in slow motion. I repeated her. She shook her head *no*. Then she reached over and took my hands in hers.

She lifted them to her face. I could feel my entire body heating up, the knuckles between my fingers stiffening. She placed them gently on her cheeks and throat.

"Feel the way I say it."

"Say it."

"Dropped."

"Draah-ppeht," I echoed her. I felt ludicrous saying it, being made to say that same word again and again. I felt like a domesticated parakeet. I cleared my head. I couldn't second-guess myself now. I felt like I was on the brink of learning some forbidden knowledge, standing on the precipice of this giant mountain that was going to be the rest of my life.

"Once more," Devin said, smiling at me. "Say it."

"Again?" I asked.

Devin nodded.

"When I move, you move," she said. My hand tensed into her cheek. She squeezed my fingers, enthusiastically, supportively. Her mouth convulsed, danced through the word like a ballerina in slow motion, voguing and pirouetting each step in one one-hundredth of normal speed, slowed down beyond the range of any normal household DVD player, moving and reacting to every microsyllable in the word.

I said it again. The moment felt like hours in my head, every part of every sound. My mouth imitated hers. For the merest

54

fraction of a second, my mouth *became* hers, more vivid than a 3-D movie, more intimate than making out. And it sounded, it *felt*, absolutely perfect.

"Just like that?" I asked her.

She smiled. "Just like that."

The moment felt perfect, the stars and planets and even passing meteors in total alignment. It was so intimate that I wondered whether we were supposed to make out. The whole idea of making out was still a foreign notion to me, and I was still unclear on the details of its choreography — was it a single moment when both involved parties felt a sudden, unavoidable rush of hormones at the same time? Was it something that both of you had to have in the back of your minds the whole time, darkly hinted at through the course of your conversation, and as soon as one person was too overt and crossed the line, you both erupted into passionate kisses and feeling-upness? Or did it just happen when we ran out of things to talk about?

I wondered if I was supposed to make the first move.

Devin reached out and grabbed hold of a guy's shoulder. A tall, well-built, muscular guy who, at rough approximation, was twice my size. He was one of the jocks who had been rough-housing around the keg, trying to out-stupid a bunch of other, identical jocks in front of the soccer girls. For a second, I thought Devin was going to tell him that I wasn't allowed to be here and ask him to take me out back and beat me up. Then I reconsidered, and decided that she was about to introduce him as her boyfriend, which might produce the same result.

"Hey, Reggie, this is Jupiter Glazer," she said, hugging his arm in a way I found both off-putting and nervousness-inducing. "Reg, Jupiter came here with Crash Goldberg and that circus, and, in his short residency at the party, he's already outgrown them. Feel like showing him around?"

"Sure, babe," he said, kissing her on the cheek in that non-committal, mixed-sex way that popular kids do when they're trying to be adultlike, as if to say, *We can get some any time we want to, so we don't need to prove it.*

Reg wrapped one firm, worked-out muscular arm around me, leading me away. I glanced behind me toward Devin, flashing her a quizzical expression. Suspicion loomed in my head that she was just trying to get rid of me.

As if she could hear my thoughts, she shook her head, and the curls at the ends of her hair shook in agreement. She mouthed the words at me, "Work your accent," and winked before turning away to address a crowd of short-skirted girls. I couldn't help but wonder why she couldn't have introduced me to them instead.

"So, Jupe," said Reg, once we were clear, "what have you been up to, and how the hell did you wind up at one of Devin's social drink-a-ramas?"

Reg Callowhill! Oh, oh, whoa. In all the madness of the crowd that was Devin Murray, I hadn't even realized who she was talking to — Reg Callowhill, who used to be my Frisbee partner in the JCC community kindergarten. When we were five, we were unbelievably tight. We had each other's backs like old-school gangsta rappers. The next year, his parents sent him to private school, and I was left to flounder by myself in Wilson Goode Elementary School. Since then, Reg had moved on to bigger and better while I had somehow managed to stay true to my loser roots.

For some reason, there was no question in my head about

opening up to him. I hadn't drunk anything, but I was feeling giddy anyway.

"I don't," I babbled to him. "I live right around here, and one of my friends got wind of the party, and my parents were screwing with me — for a change — and I was just, like, what the hell. I can jump right out my window, you know? I just needed to escape. I mean, this has been practically the worst week ever — I just started at North Shore —"

"Whoa, no way! You're at North Shore? I just transferred out of Blessed Sacrament. I'm at North Shore, too!"

I was about to say, *No duh, Reg — in case you haven't noticed, you're already in line to be King of the School, and the rest of the students only think I'm important when the person who's beating me up is important.* But then I realized that if he hadn't heard any news of my run-ins with Bates, it was actually a good sign. Maybe my reputation, as carcinogenic as it had been to start out, was not etched in stone for all eternity.

"Here," he was saying, "let me show you around. That's Crash Goldberg. You know him, I guess — Crash, get your hands off her, she's gay! — and these are the guys. Guys, this is Jupiter. He's cool, so treat him good. Hey, somebody get him a beer?"

In a few minutes, I was playing it totally cool, beer in hand, telling wildly entertaining stories about my exploits over the first week of school and my adventures hanging out in the Yards. Because they were drunk, they all thought every word I said was the funniest, most diabolically clever thing in the universe. Because I wasn't, I kept on top of the game, keeping them laughing, making sure they were never laughing at me. I was only pretending to sip my beer — not because I was a prude or anything, but because I didn't really trust myself to get drunk in a room full of potential hazards to my physical being. My parents had raised me on mother's milk and vodka, and if there was one thing I knew how to do right at this party, it was to carry my alcohol.

These jocks were seeming alright, but, you know, I didn't need to push it. Finally, one of them slapped me on the back, laughing so hard he was wheezing, and said, "Jupiter, you are the greatest. I don't even know *why* you're the greatest but you *are*, man. You tell that Bates punk, if he ever messes with you, he's gonna have to deal with us, you know?"

"Uh . . . yeah," I said uncertainly. "I know."

And then everybody laughed, and everyone raised their beer mugs high, and everyone but me swilled a giant, football-team-size gulp.

The truth was, I wouldn't depend on any of these guys to leap to my side in a fight. I barely trusted them to remember me by Monday morning. If Bates did lay into me, and any of Reg's friends came upon it, I doubted very much that anyone but me would sustain the worst of the damage. But I appreciated the sentiment, and I was enjoying being the center of the crowd and having people actually listen to me. At some point over the course of the evening, I remember catching Devin's eye — she was mostly engaged in flirting with the lead singer of a local punk band, which, in my newly social state, I didn't mind at all — and she just nodded approvingly at me, as if to say, *You finally got it, Jupiter.*

I have to say, this whole not-having-an-accent thing was definitely agreeing with me.

Later that night, a gang of guys in North Yardley High jackets showed up, prematurely ending the party when they tried to forcibly abduct the keg and roll it out to their pickup truck. Someone began screaming that someone had a gun. The screaming got everyone scattering, and the frenzied snatches of conversation — "A gun?" "A gang broke in!" "Where'd our ride go??" — spread the panic like an airborne disease. At first I tried to ignore it, since people were talking to me and I was actually having a good time. But the crowd got smaller and smaller as the non-Yards folks edged away from the newcomers and made excuses to leave. The fighting over the keg rose in tone and volume. One of Devin's guy friends was trying to make them stop; they pushed him around like a rag doll. Finally, one of the guys just decided to tip it over. The keg hit the floor with a bang, and someone yelled out "Guns!" and then I found myself suddenly using my amazing new accent to talk to no one but the air.

I decided that maybe it was time for me to make my exit.

I began to head casually to the door where everyone else was stampeding. I knew from the Yards that gangs never went after the people who weren't panicking; if you didn't think you were in trouble, they, more often than not, weren't about to give it to you. For a second, I felt like my old self, and the idea that my Yards-ness was something I could turn off and on, like a mute button or email encryption, both enthralled and terrified me.

About halfway to the door, something made me stop and turn around.

The Yardley gang was in full effect now, moving the keg out the door, getting down to the music that lingered on the turn-tables, a bizarrely hip-sounding remix of a They Might Be Giants song. It seemed not to match the actual scene unfolding: the room almost empty, all movement either slowed down or completely stopped, the Yardley guys looking fiercely triumphant. Three of them were bent over the keg, wheeling it in some way. Two more followed around Devin, who was whispering to her friends, presumably trying to convince them not to leave. A few others were clustered around, draining the remains of the bar and having a good time. One Yardley guy was necking hard-core with a girl against the bar, clawing his dirty hands under her leather jacket and all over her white tank top. He backed off, fumbling for a half-full glass on the bar, and the girl pushed her peroxide-blond hair out of her face.

I grinned wryly, almost knowing who I'd see. Her eyes, almost at once upon pulling away from the guy, focused on me.

It wasn't such a surprise. I mean, I was almost alone, one of the last remaining North Shore kids at the party. I didn't have an hour's ride back home, I didn't have to hustle a ride to my neighborhood, and, of course, I didn't know any good after-parties. My shadow cast across the length of the warehouse floor by those rented house-party lights, the solitary figure left where I was standing, and the only target for the eyes of a girl coming out of a hot and heavy make-out session.

"What up, kid?" she said, almost a whisper, although I could hear it all the way across the warehouse.

I smiled back.

"What up, Margie?" I said, in my new downtown voice, exactly the same tone as hers. I knew her name wasn't Margie, but I said it anyway. I think she got it.

And that's how I lost my accent.

5. HOW I LOST MY ACCENT

didn't lose it for good. Not immediately, at least.

If my decision to drop my accent was a science fair project, then Friday night would have been my hypothesis statement, and the weeks that followed were the rest of it, the experimentation and research and the cutting and pasting to make my diorama look like it deserved an A.

In other words: I had to start learning how to sell myself.

I took all my parents' old records. I went on a rampage on the turntable, discarding the antiquated '50s country and lounge-singer albums that they'd bought at thrift stores while they looked for their hair-core records, love ballad after love ballad, and selecting only the most passably retro records — James Brown, Johnny Hartman, Frank Sinatra, and the immortal Sammy Davis Jr.

Then I went out to the thrift store and ransacked their bargain bin for the best it had to offer. I listened to The B-52's, The Beach Boys, Dire Straits, The Cure. I listened to each of the singers, mouthed the words (first with the lyric sheet, then without) and I gleaned from them the person I wanted to be. I plagiarized syllables, vocabulary words, and the breaths and spaces in between, integrating them all into my voice. Every hour of every day, I was either listening to someone or I was listening to my headset, to the little yellow Walkman that I'd picked up for a dollar thirty-five at the local Salvation Army, to the tapes from long ago and to the voices that I wanted to be. The batteries cost more than the Walkman did, but people paid thousands of dollars to get the education I was receiving. Really, I thought, what I was getting was priceless: an open ticket to not getting beat up ever, ever again.

That weekend, I prepared for the rest of my life. It was going to be Easy Street, but it was the hardest Easy Street I'd ever heard of. I was challenging my own biology, trying to will my lips to change shape, my tongue to dance differently.

Monday morning, when I emerged from my room, my parents were both sitting at the kitchen table, drinking individual cups of coffee. They both drank instant coffee, strong, but they drank it sparingly. When both of them were *sitting down* and drinking *full cups*, you knew it was bad.

They didn't say anything when I ran through, my customary mad dash to make it to the bus stop in time for the 7:35. I glanced over my shoulder for a second and saw their faces. Their looks tore through me like I was old newspaper.

The looks said, *What happened?* and *Why us?* and *We don't know you anymore.*

I hate to say it — I hated, actually, to even *think* it — but it actually felt pretty cool.

*   *   *

Vadim wasn't at his usual bus stop — he'd come in early for his meeting with Principal Mayhew — and the 18 bus chugged along slower than ever, but I had my headphones on, and the ride felt like the fastest in recent memory. I listened to the lead singer of The Cure, who the coffee-stained booklet referred to as Robert Smith, as he sang about loss and anguish and giant spiders eating his head, which I initially decided was a bit of slang so fresh that I didn't even understand it. I vowed to start working it into my conversations . . . until I realized that the tape was even older than I was, and for all the wonders this was doing for my pronunciation, maybe I had better just chill out and wait on the snappy dialogue until I started eavesdropping on my peers to make sure it was current.

But the truth was, I didn't have to say anything. From the moment I stepped through the metal detector that morning, everything felt different. Maybe the scowls of disapproval had faded along with the freshness of the first day of school, or maybe everyone had found something new to be angsty about. I no longer felt the constant urge to stuff myself into a locker and hide.

The first person I saw on my morning walk was Crash Goldberg, the kid with all the explosions. He was hanging out with a bunch of people who looked like the cast of a horror movie, the *after* cast — pale skin, hair like electric shocks, fake (?) blood dribbling from the corners of their mouths. They were lurking in a corner by the front doors, tossing safety pins and coins through the metal detector as kids they didn't like passed through. Crash spotted me at once and gave me a little salute. "Mornin', Jupiter," he said, straight-faced.

The other guys waved.

Whoa.

I kept walking, speeding up just in case they were planning anything. But they weren't. I listened for someone coming after me, but there was nothing. Halfway down the hallway, I looked over my shoulder and they were getting ready to chuck an alarm clock through the metal detector as a really snobby-looking girl headed inside.

I smiled to myself. Not only did I not get punked by Crash, but I was actually starting to see the humor in high school pranks. Was I finally fitting in to school, or was I going insane? Maybe both, I figured.

At the end of the first-floor hallway, I passed the doors leading to the South Lawn. This was where all the Satanic people hung out — the goths and the punks and the death-metal kids and the kids who weren't part of any clique but just liked to hang out with people as bloodthirsty as they were. Even before I'd started at North Shore, people had warned me about the kids on the South Lawn. They'd allegedly slipped Rohyphol into the teachers' coffee the morning of finals and locked them inside the lockers of honor students. They'd killed baby goats on Friday afternoons, when classes were done. They'd rolled freshmen down the hill in garbage cans, then forced them to be Satan's slaves.

This morning, the doors were wide open.

A bunch of goths stood out there, smoking clove cigarettes. They stood in the perfect direction to let the smoke filter into the school. A bunch of guys in army fatigues were standing around a tree, doubtlessly planning something sinister, probably involving goat blood. Then I caught a glimpse of Bates sitting calmly on the South Lawn stairs, cradling his staff in his arms. I guess everything had turned out okay for him.

I hurried off. My encounter with Crash had me feeling pretty okay about my social standing, but I didn't want to push it too far.

Then, in the stairwell, I ran into Reg Callowhill. He was walking with a bunch of upperclassmen from the lacrosse team. They were all dressed in matching jackets, all tossing balls at each other like one complicated juggler with many disembodied arms. Clearly, he'd be joining them soon.

"Hey, Jupiter," he said, slapping me five on my way up and their way down the stairs.

"Hey," I replied breathlessly.

Then the chorus came, a panoply of *heys* and *yos* and *what's ups*. I lingered on the last step, frozen in confusion. Had I met them all at Devin's party? Or were they just going along with Reg, being cool with whoever he thought was cool in a kind of A equals B postulate of acceptability?

Then again — what difference did it make?

All morning, it went like that. Kids I didn't know stopped me in the hallway. Kids I vaguely recognized from the party had conversations with me about subjects I didn't even pretend to understand, movies I'd never heard of and MTV bands I'd never heard of and girls I'd never heard of. Several of them asked me if I remembered what had happened to them at the end of the party — and when I said no, they were duly impressed. "Wow, you must have been even more wasted than I was," cooed this one girl, as I imagined her fingers casually winding and unwinding the curls on my head. Without bothering to wait for my answer, she replied, "Damn, dude — you are *on* it," and then turned around in her seat just in time for the teacher to call on her. She got the question wrong, but man, was I glowing.

Meanwhile, Vadim was having his own case of the Mondays. Just as he'd been told to, he'd showed up to Dr. Mayhew's office at 7:45, exactly half an hour before the first bell of the day. He'd knocked three times on the frosted-glass door, just below the embossed letters of Dr. Mayhew's name. Then he'd stepped back and waited. He'd clutched his books tightly to his chest, ready to hand them back to Dr. Mayhew in a second — ready, as it were, to exchange them for the set of books applicable to the next grade up. The expression on his face (I'm imagining this part) must have been tentative, anticipatory, eager. Vadim had been moved up twice before, but never at a high school where simply being there was already a privilege. His hands must have trembled, anticipating Dr. Mayhew's inviting look. His eyes must have never left the glass door.

He stood there for five minutes.

Finally, the door opened. Dr. Mayhew was just taking off his hat and jacket, ready to jump into the day. He looked vaguely disoriented as he gazed upon the impossibly small boy who stood at his door, gazing back up at him with the expectation of salvation in his eyes.

"Uh," he said. "Can I help you?"

"I'm Vadim Khazarimovsky," Vadim reminded him. "We spoke on Friday about my classes being too easy?"

If Vadim expected that fact to jog the principal's memory, warm him up, and make them instant pals, it didn't work. It did, however, jog his memory. Dr. Mayhew peered at him through half-lidded eyes, as if sizing him up.

"Sir?" said Vadim, still hopeful.

"Ah," Dr. Mayhew said, itching his chin, faint with stubble. "The upstart. Yes, well, it's good you've got your books out — image, my boy, image. Let me take you somewhere."

I was jonesing in the hallway, waiting for class to begin, when Devin Murray marched straight up to me, a stack of flyers in her hand. She didn't even make a pretense of pretending to be too busy to talk to me until I initiated the conversation. How cool was that? She was so popular, she didn't even have to make a thing out of being popular.

"Hey, Jupiter," she said, smiling her ultra-lipsticked smile. "Good to see you. How'd you enjoy the party?"

"It was — man, I can't even tell you, Devin," I said, gushing earnestness at her. "Thanks so much for having me. It was really cool of you."

"Glad you came," Devin replied airily. "Anyway, you don't know anyone who lives in the Yards, do you?"

I almost choked on the *yes* that was about to spring from my throat, forcing it back down to the depths of my esophagus with a discipline that bordered on superhuman. "I don't think so," I said cagily, being careful to avoid that outright *no*, "but I can ask around."

"Would you? That would be so cool, thanks!" She spun around a hundred and eighty degrees on one of those three-inch heels of hers, completed a quick about-face, and continued on her morning walk.

My hand jumped up of its own accord, and I felt myself

getting ready to reach after her. I didn't want her to leave. I wanted her to stay in the hall and talk to me for twenty more seconds, so maybe another forty people could pass us and realize my new status of acceptability. That would certainly erase the whole Bates thing from their consciousnesses.

"Why do you ask?" I choked out suddenly.

Of all the things I could have asked, that might not have been the worst. But it was definitely — *definitely* — the most potentially incriminating.

Devin stopped in midstride, turned around, and tilted her head to the side.

"That group of kids who trashed the party," she said. "They stole the beer keg, remember? Well, Nessa Greyscole still owes her parents three hundred dollars from the deposit."

"Three hundred dollars?!"

"It was the biggest keg they had. And we would've finished it, too, if it wasn't for that gang," she said. "Anyway, if you see any white-trash kids floating around the school who look familiar, let me know. Here, take one of these."

She handed me a flyer.

It was Photoshopped to look like a Wanted sign from the Old West, complete with old block letters and a reward. In the space where the mug shot was supposed to go, there was a picture of a toxic waste dump. "'Wanted: Low-Down, Dirty Keg Thieves and Stool Pigeons,'" I read aloud. "And she's offering a three hundred dollar reward? Why doesn't she just use the money to pay the deposit?"

"I'm offering the reward myself," Devin informed me, already looking down the corridor to find more people to hit up. "I figure it's my civic duty and all. I mean, I *did* convince her to lay out the cash in the first place."

I thought about suggesting an alternate plan, but decided to keep silent. "Whoa," I said. It was, I thought, what popular kids said when they didn't know what else to say.

"Nessa said that Reg said that Crash said that someone saw one of the Yards gang looking tight with one of the people at the party," she informed me, the valley-girl tone in her voice suddenly gone. "One of *our* people. Reg reckons they told the Yards guys to come over and crash the party. I seriously can't imagine — I mean, why would anyone from the Yards even *be* at the party in the first place? — but, you know, they had to find out about it somehow. That's the stool pigeon part."

"Maybe they were just cruising by?" I suggested.

"Maybe," Devin echoed dryly — as though she wouldn't believe it for a second. "Anyway, thanks for listening. It's good to see you in action, you know? I mean, within the walls of North Shore and everything."

"Yeah," I started to say, "you, too," but Devin was already cruising down the hall, removing the next flyer from the top of the pile.

Dr. Mayhew led Vadim down the first-floor hallway. They whizzed past students digging in their lockers, students sitting against classroom doors and studying, students talking and flirting and hurrying to wherever they had to go. Dr. Mayhew moved faster than them all. They say that a school is only as good as the principal that leads it, and in the case of North Shore, both school and principal were irrevocably intertwined — so much so that it seemed to Vadim that the hallways flexed and curved with each of Mayhew's steps. When they banked sharply to the left to avoid the hip-hop kids who were freestyling in the center of the corridor, the walls themselves seemed to bend left to allow them free passage.

Finally, they stopped in front of a short stairwell that seemed to lead nowhere. Through its dim, cobwebby top, Vadim could see a rusted brass sign on the door, a door that hadn't been opened in years, that read JANITOR'S CLOSET — NO ADMITTANCE.

Up and down along the stairs, though, sat a good dozen or so of the smartest, geekiest, most socially unaware and fashionably clueless ninth-through-twelfth-graders that Vadim had ever set his 45/20-prescription eyes upon.

They were all genders, but mostly male; all races, but their skin glowed with the uniform mint green sheen of those people who derived most of their light from a computer screen, rather than from the sun. The four kids highest up the stairs were clustered around the new English edition of the Dead Sea Scrolls, fighting over a mistake in translation. Two steps down from them, a girl of unspeakable beauty swept her fingers over her computer keyboard, a dirty red landscape on the screen, calculating the odds of recurring fractal patterns on the surface of Mars. At the bottom of the stairs, four people were actively engaged in a yelling match over what looked to Vadim like the most violent, heatedly intense, full-contact game of Scrabble he had ever seen. Dr. Mayhew didn't even have to open his mouth; Vadim was already sold. At that moment, the principal could have told Vadim to jump off a bridge, and Vadim would only have asked at what trajectory he should hit the water.

Dr. Mayhew, never one to linger in a moment, cleared his throat.

The Scrabblers froze mid-spelling, looked up from the board, and rotated their heads north.

"Consuela Cortez," Dr. Mayhew said. Even in his regular speaking voice, everything sounded like an announcement. "Would you mind coming forward?"

From the hazy heights of the top of the staircase, a heavy, suspicious-looking girl, her hair neatly swirled in the shape of a question mark from the back of her head all the way down to the small of her back, descended.

"Yeah?" she said, sounding bored. "What do you want, Mayhew?"

"This," boomed Dr. Mayhew, ignoring the obvious besmirching of his title, "is Vadim. He's a first-year student. I think he might be able to find his place among you. I'd appreciate it if you could take him under your wing, show him the ropes, mind that he doesn't take off in the —" he cleared his throat "— in the wrong direction."

Consuela continued her slow, laborious descent until she was standing opposite Vadim. He was small by anyone's standard, not making it up to most people's line of sight, but to Consuela, he was barely a blip. His tiny head just barely reached the bottom curvature of her breasts. At that moment, his eyeballs were currently rotating upward, coming into an eventual contact with her downward-orbiting eyes. Through the double layers of glasses that shielded both their sets of eyes, they made slow contact.

"Vadim," she grunted. "What's your deal?"

"Hey," Vadim said, speaking slowly and carefully. "I'm trying to get out of this place. I got kicked out of Decanometry on the first day 'cause our teacher said to graph a ten-dimensional plane, and I tried to launch a tesseract into the equation."

Consuela let out a low whistle.

That was when Vadim noticed it. All the activity that had ceased when he'd first arrived hadn't picked back up again. Everyone's eyes were on him. Everyone was analyzing him, trying to see how he'd slip up.

What he'd just said, that was what they were waiting for.

"*Niiice,*" cooed a voice from the top of the stairs. "Factoring by way of tesseract. Most kids are into Deco, or they're into *A Wrinkle in Time*, but the overlap is where it counts."

That came from the girl with the Martian surface on her laptop. Having made her opinion known, she lowered her eyes back to her laptop screen, adjusted the collar of her shirt, and continued working.

That girl, Vadim would soon learn, was Cynthia Yu, an absolutely brilliant fourteen-year-old behavioral mathematician who passed her summers at the University of Pennsylvania's Artificial Intelligence department.

Right now, Vadim didn't pay too much attention to the messenger. I knew that all he needed to hear was that he was approved of. Then his blood pressure would lower, and his heart would stop thudding against his ribcage and return to its normal rhythm.

Consuela, similarly satisfied, wrapped her arm around his shoulders and started introducing him around. From that moment on, Vadim didn't care about skipping another grade, transferring schools, or what his Decanometry teacher thought of him. He'd found a community, and that — for now, at least — was all that mattered.

Between fourth and fifth periods, I looked up in the hallway and saw Bates's staff drifting above the crowd. I worked up the courage to approach him about it.

"Hey, Bates," I said, flashing him my friendliest smile. "Good to see you all freshly re-staffed. How you doin'?"

He threw me against the closest locker. The metal slits dug into my spinal cord. His forearm tightened like a knot around my Adam's apple, and I felt the staff wedged in the unbearably narrow area between my ear and the rest of my head.

"I'm sorry," he said. "You want to run that by me again??"

I winced. When someone squashes your neck from the front, your first instinct, no matter what, is to pull back. Even if pulling back means digging yourself even harder into a sharply molded locker with jagged points that push hard into your skin, more painful than your assailant's choking hold.

"*Mister* Bates!" came the familiar monotone of Dr. Mayhew's voice from down the hall. "We've received those Freedom of Religion pamphlets for you from the ACLU. Congratulations again on your recent victory. . . ."

The tone of his voice deepened, got lower and grew more suspicious as he saw Bates holding me in such a compromising position. But Bates's hold loosened as he turned around and I managed to slip out and duck into the oncoming tide of students. I massaged my neck, looking around to see whether anyone had noticed the newest assault on my dignity.

Then I heard a squeal and turned to see the girls' soccer

team waving at me. The bitter taste in my mouth suddenly tasted a lot like candy.

The first day or two of being popular — no, let's not get ahead of ourselves. The first day of not looking like a punching bag was pretty dizzyingly amazing. After that, it was just dizzying. Wednesday afternoon, I spotted Sajit coming out of the girls' bathroom, surrounded by a throng of stomach-sucking soccer-team girls, all bouncing in one communal laugh. He caught my eye, twisted out of the crowd, and matched my pace.

"*Juuu*piter," he crooned in that way only he said my name. "I keep hearing all these *things* about you, man. How come it's all in the third person?"

"Which third person?"

"From *other* people, you fnord. You're quite the celebrity, you know. Your name is on the girls' bathroom wall. You've officially become one of the popular kids."

I grinned. I couldn't help it, I was really impressed with myself. "Really? What does it say?"

"Oh, nothing. Just a phone number that isn't really yours. But how are you doing? How does it feel?"

The grin flickered for a second. Sajit noticed it; not much slipped beneath his radar. "What does that mean?"

"Well . . ." I hesitated. I couldn't help it — I never liked to spoil a surprise, or to point out that part in the movie where you could see the overhead microphone, and I felt way guilty questioning my blessings.

He nodded me on.

"It's great that I'm not getting laughed at by the those kids anymore," I said. "But, since when did I ever start *liking* them?"

We both stopped in our tracks. It was a difficult question, and a valid one.

But Sajit had always been the master of positive thinking. Ever since first grade, when he tore open the ice packs that we nursed our black eyes with and discovered that you could suck the ice, he had his own way of looking at things. "Don't knock the hustle," he said simply. "You don't have to play the game. Just enjoy sitting at the top of the board."

And that was that.

From where I stood, my newfound popularity was definitely tasting better than my old lack of it, but, oddly enough, I wasn't feeling at all satisfied. By the end of the week, it had started to feel as though everyone on the attendance list of North Shore High had said hi to me, but I still hadn't managed to have one decent conversation — with the exception of Devin Murray, who it seemed like I now had to avoid. The less she found out about me, where I came from and where I currently resided, the better.

The last period bell rang. Mr. Denisof talked straight through its blanketing shrill, but we gathered up our books and jammed them into our backpacks. "Read chapters three and four, answer all the odd-numbered questions, and, Jupiter Glazer, don't think I've forgotten you," he announced, seemingly oblivious to the tide of students running past him and through the door.

"Sir?" I was still stuck in my seat.

"You might think you're smart, waltzing right back in like nothing happened. But I've got my eye on you," he told me. "I would advise you not to forget that."

I gave a summary nod, zipped my backpack shut, and ran

out. I didn't know what sort of veiled threats he was intimating, but I knew I couldn't think about it anymore. From the time first period started at 8:16, I'd gone through six hours and forty-five minutes of consecutive thinking. I needed to give my brain a break.

So that's what I did. Outside, there was a stream of kids making their way from the front doors to the bus stop, a single huge wave that seemed to grow into a pool that mobbed each passing bus, flowing into its doors. The crowd going toward the Yards seemed surprisingly crowded, given both that it had a reputation for being the dumbest neighborhood in the city and that Devin couldn't seem to find anyone at our school who actually lived there.

I'd been dealing with crowds all day. Another pack of hungry and horny teenagers was not what I felt like experiencing right now.

I turned around, thinking I'd climb back up the hill and back into school, see if anyone was doing anything remotely interesting, since now I didn't have a job to get back to. Maybe I would try to track down Vadim.

All those thoughts vanished in the moment I set my eyes on the door.

Standing there, a bit like a lion trying to decide which herd to hunt down first, chest puffed out, long hair blowing in the wind, was Bates, twirling his pointed staff over his head.

I retreated. One foot behind the other, slowly. If you didn't move fast or act afraid, lions wouldn't pounce on you, right? No, that was snakes. Lions weren't blind. Lions could see fear, smell fear, watch fear eat at your nerves and your vital

76

organs until you were a cowering, blubbering mass trying to act cool and back away. Then, like a lazy Sunday afternoon decision, they would leap on you and rip you to pieces with their pinkie claw.

That was how Bates was looking at me right now.

I glanced behind me, looking for the huge crowd that would swallow me up. It was twenty or thirty feet away. Bates's staff had stopped orbiting above his head. Now he held it like a spear, pointing at me.

His mouth drew open with a piercing, throaty, guttural yell.

Really? I thought.

Which was when he started to run straight at me.

I ran, too. My backpack bouncing off my back, the curls of my hair whacking in my eyes, pavement, turf, and unmowed grass fell beneath my feet. I tasted wind. Bates had managed to chase me on a diagonal, away from the after-school mass, and my sudden gratitude at not being publicly shamed was now holding a distant second to my desperate, agonizing wish for a crowd to hide in. He chased me through the empty sports field, past the swinging unlocked doors, through the hole in the fence. Across the street from the school was a row of shady-looking high-rise apartments, the kind mostly known for being backdrops for crime shootings on prime-time TV.

There was a red light. I ran across five lanes of stopped traffic. Bates jumped off the curb, giving another war whoop, his staff ready to harpoon.

I reached the far side. There was a barbed-wire fence surrounding the shady apartments. Great — I wasn't even allowed *in*. I glanced around, looking for something to hide behind.

And then I saw the bus.

And then the light turned green.

I hammered on the door. From the line of windows, the people who were already on the bus stared disdainfully down at me. The driver's head swung toward me, pissed, then reached over to swing the door open. "Alright, but I'm not doing this every day," he griped as I climbed on.

I dropped in my token, grateful for the opportunity to continue my natural life span, and collapsed into an empty seat.

I turned to the man next to me, a tough-looking bald man in a plaid shirt with no sleeves. Mustering the last leftovers of my Friday-night charisma, I smiled at him and asked, "What direction is this bus going in?"

He looked at me like I was crazy.

"Downtown," he said.

Downtown was a whole other world. A million cars chugged slowly down streets, and a thousand people swarmed around you at any given moment. The sidewalks were too impossibly small for the amount of people that were populating them. You felt like you needed to move, to move in time with the human conveyor belt around you, or else become trapped in the onslaught, crushed into a grate. Downtown was busy, deliciously busy. People watching was not just for those of us who lived in the margins of society. You almost didn't have a choice — you *had* to stare. Downtown was like spacewalking — your feet never touched the ground, and your hands, when you twitched them, felt aware, dangerously aware, that there was nothing that lay between them and the open depths of outer space, just empty air that could suck you out of your clothes at any moment, catapulting you into forever.

The bus pulled up right into a terminal near City Hall. I climbed off the back doors, skated down the stairs, and sprung, feetfirst, into the crowd.

I had no destination. I had no deadline — well, not unless you counted factory work, which I didn't anymore. I had no plans, except to walk around, maybe get a coffee, and check out the center of the city that had taken half my life.

It really did feel like landing on another planet. It's not like I'd never been downtown — my parents used to take me every year for the Fourth of July and the New Year's parades — but I'd never felt it out in terms of being an actual city.

Chestnut Street felt just like the movies, homely Colonial trees leisurely draped across buildings, their brick walls a red as fresh as just-cooked bread. It was four or so in the afternoon, too early for businesses to let out, but a few businesspeople crawled the streets anyway, window-shopping and laughing with unseen spouses on their cell phones.

Most people I was watching, though, were of another caliber entirely.

The first one I noticed was a girl. Tall, thin, with impossibly long and stringy hair, she was wearing all black, but her clothes were varied enough in style and texture, a tweed black vest over a shiny black shirt, so they didn't even look all black. She was older than me, but only by a few years, her skin still fresh and soft and unwrinkled, her iPod sticking out from a pocket of her vest. I watched her go by, not checking her out, more just staring in awe of her. It was so cool. I'd never judged a person by their clothes before, but her clothes were so cool, it was impossible not to. She was the kind of person, I decided in a flash, that I could grow up to be.

She passed me in her flurry of a walk, disappeared inside a record store a few buildings down. I debated following her in — and do what? Stalk her? — but life didn't give me a chance. I spotted a whole group (of kids? people? girls and guys together?) walking along the other side of the street. I ducked between two cars, trailed behind them for a block or so, following as they cut along side streets, walked in the middle, ignoring cars and traffic lights. The whole time, they were talking about this book they'd all read.

I'd read that book last year.

At the time, I'd wanted to talk about it with someone, with anyone, but I couldn't find anyone in the Yards who'd even heard of it. I'd sat Vadim down, expecting him to at least listen to me, but when I told him, he was like, "What do you want to tell me about a book for?" If they didn't have comics or quantum theory in them, Vadim said, you might as well just hide books in a library where nobody would ever read them.

I lost track of them and of their conversation about the time we crossed onto a small street where winding ivy blanketed all the buildings like camouflage. There was a tiny coffeehouse about halfway down, drenched in the wafting scents of smoke and ground coffee beans. The few vacant tables outside (it was starkly warm outside, still summer, but just barely) belied its packed interior. More of these creatures sat inside there, talking to one another, typing away on laptops and reading books and posing in their seats. They wore wacky, nonjudgmental clothes, goofy plaids and neon paisleys, Sherlock Holmes hats and tacky '80s belts. Each of them looked like the kind of person I could become best friends with and talk to for hours.

I wanted to find out how to start.

I went in and ordered a café au lait, very nervous when I pronounced the name. I took it, along with the fortune cookie that came on the saucer, and sat at the vacant end of a long, packed table. Café au lait was just coffee with milk, but somehow it always tasted better than when I tried pouring milk in my regular coffee — some sort of barista magic that only those professionally trained in the ways of the coffeehouse could bring about. I wanted to take out my journal and write — following the example of the plurality of the folks in the coffeehouse — but, I realized ashamedly, I didn't have a journal. I contented myself with taking out one of the spiral notebooks from my new semester of school (all our teachers wanted us to have three-ring binders, anyway) and started writing lines from my new songs in there, verses of poems I had to memorize in years past, anything I could think of to keep my hands busy. My eyes were surveying the people around me, their habits and conversations and eccentric, nonconformist ways of existing, and suddenly, thrillingly, it felt like a mission.

I wanted to learn how to be like this. Older. Independent. Untouchable.

6. FASCINATION STREET

I thought I had everything totally figured out. I kept feeling that way, right up to the second I stepped into my house.

"Jupiter, you cannot quit the work now. This is family business, and you are family. If you want to live in our house, you must pitch in to help us keep the house. You not understand that?" That was my mother. She was always yanking the umbilical cord when she needed to reel me in.

I pretended to ignore her.

That brought in the second wave of assault, my father, who was a less effective communicator but would not give up so easily. "Jupiter, you listen now! We bring you to this country! We make you good living, pay for good food. Now worst time of year for us. You need help us!"

I turned around, finally acknowledging their existence. "Look, guys," I said in the calmest, most rational voice I could muster. "I realize this is a difficult season for the operation, and you're both under a lot of pressure to perform and to succeed. And I am perfectly capable of realizing that the corporation has done us a great favor by letting us live here. I just can't manage the time right now. I'm sorry, but I really can't."

"This is no excuse, we know high school is hard but we need you."

"You don't know anything," I said. "You've never gone through this. You don't understand."

"We understand! You not understand! We understand!"

"*Mommmm —*"

"Jupiter, *viros umnik na moyu golovu —*"

This is what they did, pulling out all the stops. When they reached the limits of their English, they retreated into their native tongue.

"Mom, I don't want to —"

"*Poka tebe tvadsat odin ne ispolnitsa budesh rabotat kak milenkiy —*"

"*Stop it!*"

Whoa. That came out about fifty thousand times louder than I'd intended it to sound. Actually, the voice that came up from my trachea and out through my lips was huge and vibrating, louder than I ever thought it could go. I took a few steps back. We all took a few steps back.

But I could feel the veins in my wrist throbbing, the anger in my body still hot.

"I'm serious," I said. "Stop speaking Russian. I am *through* with that language. I'm just through with it. Never speak it to me again. If you want to yell at me, do it in English."

I waited, panting. It was this weird showdown that we hadn't known was a showdown until just now. All of a sudden, none of us was sure what to do.

After a few beats, I stopped standing there and went up to my room. I swung open my window and climbed out on the roof, savoring the cold Septemblurry air, breathing in deep gulps of freedom.

I was sitting in a used bookstore on Second Street, thinking very hard about things that felt too unimportant to waste my time thinking about — how to become independent and untouchable — but mostly, I was just loitering. It seemed like for every minute I spent in active participation with other human beings my own age, I required half an hour of time to digest and process the experience. At this exact moment I was thinking about Vadim, wondering if there was an actual mathematical equation to take someone like us — an antisocial, emotionally isolated Russian Jewish kid with no cultural background and nothing in common with anyone at our school but age — and turn him popular. Subtract sixty percent of an accent, divide by the amount of people who recognize you by sight, recalibrate into terms of a warehouse party in (everyone-but-me-wise, anyway) the middle of nowhere, and the figure that emerges will be . . . what?

Actually, that was a lie. I was curled up in an armchair big enough to hold three of me, leafing through ancient hardcover books and glazing over the words. Sometimes, I would stop on a random complicated word, *epistle* or *catatonic* or *kumquat*, and try to put it into the context of my life. I mouthed the word several times, tasted the way my gums moved. I imagined saying it to Devin Murray, to Bates, and then to Margie.

I glanced up from the book. The words were blurring together, and the language started looking way too twirly and snakelike — too much like doodles, not enough boxes. In the window, a figure hurried past in a brown-and-white restaurant uniform and a short blond bob cut.

"Margie?" I called out, forgetting the barrier of glass.

I hurried out from the store, tried to catch up with the vanishing figure, but she had already turned the corner. Meanwhile, the clerk from the store had called after me, seeing as I was still holding the book that I hadn't paid for. I sighed. Time to pull the no-speakee-the-English routine and get out of it.

"It's called *college*," Vadim said to me in school, between classes, when we finally had a chance to meet up. "You go away to college, and you start acting like that. It's all a side effect of smoking too much pot. People act crazy for a year or two, realize their parents aren't around to make sure they're dressing normal and scoring good grades, and then they either get their act together or they flunk out."

"Is that how it works?" I said. "Why are you thinking so much about college all of a sudden? I feel like it's been a year since we hung out." I checked my class schedule in my head. It was Friday when I'd gone to his house, and now it was Wednesday. Not an eon, but long enough for my life to completely change its essence and purpose.

"A year? You're so dramatic, Jupiter. I've just been up to my own stuff." He cracked a hint of a smile. "Hey, what's up with your voice?"

"My voice?" I said. I cleared my throat, gurgled my saliva, and said it again. "What's wrong with my voice?"

"Your accent," he said. "You sound like an amoeba with laryngitis. Why you are talking so funny?"

Vadim's grammar slip-ups — how did I always notice grammar

slip-ups? Was I that paranoid about my own? — were so rare an occurrence that I had to stop talking totally. I realized we were speaking English even though it was just the two of us.

"It was at the party Friday night," I said. "I was talking to this girl, and she told me —"

"You were talking? To a girl?"

I couldn't tell whether Vadim was being sarcastic or not.

"Not like *that*!" I said. "I mean, I was talking to girls all night, Vadim. I told you — you utterly should have come."

"Yeah, right," Vadim said darkly, as though I had just suggested that he donate a pint of blood to the South Lawn kids.

"But, listen. The party was nothing — it was just school kids, you know? What you *really* need to see is the life downtown."

It was like I couldn't stay away. Even though Vadim begged off (there was an Odyssey of the Mind meeting after school, or something like that), I had to plunge back in. Last time, I'd left the coffeehouse well before sunset. But this time, I wanted to stay there. I wanted to watch the hours turn.

If the night had gone on for twenty years, if the darkness stretched out forever and became the only experience I ever experienced again, it would have been enough for me. I left the coffeehouse long after dark, an eternity after school had let out.

Once again, I hadn't spoken to anyone there, other than a brief, self-conscious, spoken-into-my-chest "small house coffee." I didn't need to. Just being there, existing in a universe with them, was enough for me — at least for now. I had the rest of my life to overload myself.

There was a second dusk that only happened downtown, after nightfall, a gradual twinkling of the stars that signified the city's descent into night. It was the transition between the dinner crowds and the nighttime crowds.

This was the kind of place where Saturday nights happened every night, where people lived every night as a joyous occasion and a potential party, not just as a time to eat dinner and finish homework and text message your geeky Russian friends. They went out as a matter of principle. Nothing was a spectator sport.

My shirt was feeling thin in the rapidly cooling air; my hands were full of coffeehouse flyers that advertised events I knew I would never attend.

And I decided then, at that moment, to come back as often as I could, to walk around and exist downtown as many nights as I could sneak away. It didn't matter if all the concerts were twenty-one and over, or if the people at the cafés looked straight through me. I just wanted to be a part of their world, to absorb everything I could and find someplace that was more real and more lifelike than the Yards.

At home, I expected to find a note on my bedroom door, as was my parents' usual ritual when they were too mad at me to talk. Since I'd already told them they weren't allowed to speak to me in Russian, letter writing was the most obvious and expected tactic that they had left. I braced myself for their shaky, uneven handwriting on dollar-store Post-it notes.

Instead there was a letter, typed on an official-looking letterhead, stuck to the rusty nail that protruded from the door.

I ripped it off my door and, holding it in both hands, scanned it for meat — cutting through the big vocabulary, looking for the words that mattered. The letter was addressed to my parents, from the management company that owned our factory. It was written in thick English, in the impenetrable language of tax forms and immigrant registration documents. But it was still understandable. It said that — good news! — the market for our product was expanding and, hence, the needs of production for our factory was expected to double. They needed to install an additional assembly line, and thus, due to the increased need for space, the family currently residing there, the Glazers, might be asked to vacate their private quarters, and, just in case, they should take an inventory of all personal belongings, gather them together, and start packing up.

The trouble with being idealistic was that everything that didn't fulfill my ideals felt like a compromise. Wanting to be a down-town, bohemian, intellectual non-Yards resident was one thing, but once I got there, once I freed myself of the Yards, what was I going to do? I sat for hours in cafés with all these amazing people — I was *sure* they were amazing — but, beyond know-ing there was a bigger destiny out there for me, what was I doing? Being a musical connoisseur and talking about indie punk band concerts was great, but with no money, there was no way I could actually get *into* a concert. And I kept waiting for that girl to talk to me, that unspeakably cool girl with cello-phane eyes, cream-soda skin, and a native fluency in the love clichés of rock song lyrics, but she was really taking her time showing up.

In the meantime, North Shore was doing its best to keep me distracted.

Breasts. I was surrounded by breasts.

Indian summer hit that weekend, and on Monday, girls' clothes were coming off like old dead skin. Tank tops. Spaghetti straps. Short shorts, bodysuits, tube tops, capris. In town, girls wore all different kinds of clothes. The coffee-shop girls still weren't talking to me, but each time I walked in, I got more approving nods in my direction. Each shy smile that I flashed at a girl, I got closer and closer to becoming convinced that not only did she see it and understand its meaning, but she was one step away from coming over to talk to me, swap iPod playlists, and take me to the always-deserted downstairs seating section for a heavy, sweaty, full-on make-out session. After all, if high school girls made out all the time at school and parties, then why wouldn't college girls (at least I assumed they were in college) be into making out at coffeehouses? They dressed differently — less obviously sexily, in washed-out fall colors and loosely hanging T-shirts and cardigans — but wasn't that just because they were more slyly sexy, because they already knew what they wanted and they knew how to get it? North Shore girls were less experimental, more obvious in their intentions. The other day, Devin said hi to me and I turned in her direction and she was wearing this shirt that was basically a sports bra — you could totally see her belly button, a stomach as tight and taut as a movie screen — and I couldn't even muster the tongueular skills to say hello back.

All of this seemed to come at a fast, clashing redirection to the phantoms of intellectuality and artisticness I'd been chasing around. The other day I had spent two hours in a downtown art gallery doing not much but staring at the paintings, treating the place like it was a museum. There was a girl sitting at a desk (tied-back black hair, sleeveless dress) who kept shooting glances at me, as if to say that it wasn't a place for museumgoers like me. I found a flyer for a concert the weekend after next, this band I'd never heard of. All the flyers were made from linoleum wood-cuts, a full round moon and the silhouettes of a werewolf and a country preacher. They looked unbelievably cool.

I started to rethink Devin's invitation to watch movies with a bunch of friends Friday night, which I'd just turned down. I started to wonder if the girl of my dreams wasn't just as likely to be hiding underneath a set of perfectly globular, slightly protrusive breasts, inflated slightly by a mercilessly tight baby-tee, still olive from a lingering August tan, lurking backstage at a concert of a band called Prowler.

But first I had to get through the week.

Monday night was spent at home with my parents, the farthest scene from a Prowler concert that I can imagine. I picked at my dinner, not in the mood for it. Not in the mood for any of this.

"The warehouse it was a crazy-people place today," said my father. "Two new factory want to order from us, and we are already behind on three factory order. If we say yes, we lose the order we already have. If no, then we may not to get another chance."

"Yeah, Dad," I said, rolling my peas through the spears of a fork. "It's a conundrum."

I used the word even though I was well aware that he probably didn't know what it meant. I didn't know why he was talking about this, not with me at the table. I mean, my mom already knew all the details, and he had to know that I didn't care. And it was true; I really didn't. What was it going to affect me whether we moved to somewhere that was even colder and trashier than this? If there was anywhere in the entire city worse than this place, it was hard to imagine.

"And the owner he say, if too much business, they may need more space."

"Big deal," I said. "So, they buy another warehouse down here or something. Maybe they'll have another family move in and be the foremen of that place. Maybe they'll have a hot daughter or something, and there'll finally be someone for me to hang out with."

Wow. I couldn't believe I'd said that. The words *hot daughter* — even if my parents, with their limited English proficiency, interpreted it literally — were dangerous words, a veritable invitation to inquire into the workings of my social life. It would be just about the worst conversation topic ever . . . except maybe for the subject that we were currently talking about. It was moments like these that turned me into a believer, that had me reaching out with my mind and trying to conjure God. *Please, change the conversation topic. Please, change the conversation topic. . . .*

My mother glared sideways at me for a second, but then she put up her hand to keep me quiet. Her gaze was locked on my father.

"Vaclav, what are you talking about?" she said. "What do you mean?"

He bowed his head, staring the coleslaw on his plate head-on.

"I am thinking they will ask us to move," he said.

*　　*　　*

The next morning, I walked down the dirty, aluminum-can-lined block as usual, and waited at the graffiti-encrusted bus shelter. My parents paid next to nothing to the company for renting the warehouse, but they also earned next to nothing. It was a trade-off. They would never have a chance to earn enough to get themselves off their feet, but they would never need to, either.

The bus came. I dropped my token into the slot and probed my wallet, counting the amount of tokens I had left. Four. Two days before I would have to ask my parents for money to buy another pack. Even at the reduced rate, it was still eleven bucks a week they were paying. For me to get to school. For me to keep on living.

And, with my new little secret, I was using up bus tokens even faster.

I saw Margie four more times in the week after my coffeehouse revelation: once at a free They Might Be Giants concert at Penn's Landing; once at a different coffeehouse, leaving just as I was going in; and twice on the bus home from one of my nights out in Center City. Calling them "nights out" was a bit of an exaggeration, since I had to be home for dinner at seven, but going downtown, even for an hour or two, counted. It was enough of an escape from the Yards to count. My parents weren't taking the news from the notice well, and were talking to the management on a daily basis to try to work it out. I wanted to be as far from those conversations as possible without crossing state lines.

I couldn't be sure that it was actually Margie each time — bumping into her in the café, I'd only seen the back of her hair

92

and caught a faint whiff of a perfume that smelled like something she would wear — but it had to be her at least one of those times. Besides, actually *talking* to Margie wasn't what I was after. Right now, having a crush was enough.

Downtown life itself was fabulous. I was learning more and more about how to be an eccentric college student each day, and I hadn't even passed ninth grade. Every afternoon after school let out, I sat in one of the coffee shops or diners that lined South Street, eavesdropping on conversations to learn the language and cadence, making my single cup of coffee last for hours. I would go into the music stores, run-down independent places, their walls and windows plastered with concert posters for bands I knew nothing about, and listen to the strange music that the clerks played when nobody else was in the store. I would set myself up in one of the anonymous and dusty aisles in the back — bluegrass and old radio shows were my favorites — and sit there for hours, my eyes closed, absorbing the songs. At first it was about the lyrics, those half-swallowed, half-mumbled words of the language I was trying to learn, but the more I got into it, the more it became about the music. Every so often, I would stick my head out, walk up to the front desk, and ask one of the unspeakably knowledgeable clerks (who looked tortured and introverted so that I both identified with and lived in fear of them) the name of the band that was playing.

"Oh," they'd say casually, "it's the Dead Milkmen."

"Oh, it's Sui Generis."

"Oh, it's Flossie and the Unicorn. Why, what do you think of them?"

That last part — the question part — they never said, except in my head. It was my one wish, above everything else, that I wasn't the only human being ever to have this bonding experience with music, that someone else was just as lonely as I was, sitting one aisle over in the Cajun/zydeco section, and one day we'd meet. I'd say the first line of a Sui Generis song. Then she (it was always a she) would reply with the call-and-response next line, and we'd never stop talking for the rest of our lives.

But every time I made my mind to get up and look in the next aisle over, it was empty.

In school, I sang songs between classes, walking from one class to another. I felt cool and eccentric, batty in that way that I was so cool that I could do anything I wanted. I got stares. But, for the most part, they were *we-think-you're-alright* stares. I didn't really care about anyone who stared at me in another way.

Of course, there were the South Lawners like Bates and his cronies, who skipped classes like stones, who looked at me askew no matter what I did. I knew Bates was angry about my escape from him and his staff, but he was biding his time for a rematch, I was sure. I was lying low. I tried not to let him or the rest of them get to me. Along with most of the rest of the average kids, I walked past them as quick as I could, pretending they didn't exist. I sang the words a little softer until I was whispering, and then I whispered a little softer until I wasn't doing anything.

The whole time, I was hoping, kind of in the back of my mind, that somebody would recognize the words. *No shit!* they'd say. *Is that a Dead Milkmen song? Man, I love the Dead Milkmen. I can't believe somebody else knows —*

The only problem was, nobody else ever did.

7. INBETWEEN DAYS

"Dude," Vadim said to me one day after school, "you will not *believe* these guys."

"These guys" were his geek posse. Since I'd been escaping downtown, I hadn't really gotten an update from Vadim and his new life for a while. Now he was giving me the full-blast catch-up. It was his only real acknowledgment that it had been a while since he'd seen me on the bus home.

"Between them, it's, what do you say, a whole *cavalcade* of knowledge. They're, like, a superhero team. This one girl, she does freelance work for the CIA because she is an insanely good hacker. They don't even know she's too young. All she had to do was give herself a Social Security number for cashing her checks. Another girl is plotting the entire surface of Mars using fractal geometry. It's a whole culture of nerds. And it doesn't even matter that I don't speak good English. This guy Felix, he came over from Brazil three and a half years ago, and still doesn't speak a word of English. But his math skills are so phenomenal that the administration doesn't kick him out, they just let him take six periods a day of math. Everyone's like that. They're all like that. And they're tough, too. When Freshman Day comes, the South Lawn won't touch these guys at all. Now I officially have a free ticket out of getting beat up when everyone else is getting beat up. So what do you think? Isn't that amazing?"

Vadim sat on the edge of the swivel chair in his room, expectant, his mouth hanging open, waiting for me to respond.

"Did you call me *dude*?" I said.

"Jupiter, did you listen at all to me?"

"Yeah, utterly. You know someone in the CIA, right?"

"*Juuu*piter . . ."

"I'm sorry, I'm sorry," I said. I actually *was* feeling bad. "Look — I really *am* interested in your new world at school, but the truth is, I can't stop thinking about downtown. Listen, Vadim, I need to tell you. It's like a whole new —"

"And another thing," Vadim said without blinking, as if I hadn't interrupted him at all. "I think I like this girl."

Conversation stop.

When I was ten and Vadim was eight — back when he was only one grade below me — he liked this girl. He liked her so much, he figured out how to reprogram the standardized test machine in our school so that everyone but her would fail completely, and she'd get a hundred. He did this a week before Valentine's Day, and then, when they were waiting outside the principal's office, he informed her of the intention behind his gesture.

She whacked him in the chin with her mini-handbag, walked out without another word, and then got Butch Warrington, the biggest, meanest, smelliest kid in school — who was also her boyfriend at the time — to chase him home every day for the next week.

That was one of Vadim's easier pursuits in the world of girls.

Neither Vadim nor I was what one would refer to as desirable. We didn't have a lot of friends, we had bad haircuts, and we both spoke poor English (well, until recently we both did). But that didn't stop us from wanting. For my own part, I played my cards cool and sparingly, mostly resigned to the wild fantasies that leaped through my brain, in one hemisphere and out the other. But Vadim, for all his knowledge in the higher disciplines, could never bring himself to admit that he was utterly clueless in the realm of carnal knowledge.

I listened as he told me about his newest daydream. Her name was Cynthia, and she was the girl who was plotting out coordinates on the Martian surface. She hadn't actually spoken to him yet, but he was already figuring out a way to make the newest round of NASA satellite photographs spell out their names.

As he talked, I started thinking about my new popularity, the fact that I was now friends — or, at least, on speaking terms — with the most popular girl in ninth grade. I thought how easily I had made friends at the party, and how contagious that popularity was.

But the truth was, I didn't want to be popular. If I *was*, I wouldn't complain, but being cool and acceptable and approachable in everyone's minds didn't have much value for me. What I wanted, what I was ultimately after — what my fantasies were about — was something greater.

I wanted to be wild.

"So, what do you think?" Vadim was saying. "Will you meet her for me?"

"Will I what?" I was lost.

"Exactly," he said. "Come to the steps with me. We can hang out with my new friends, and you will check her out. You can tell her good things about me, see if you think she's worth, you know, getting to know. Just try to see if you can tell what she thinks of me. You're good with people, Jupiter. Do you think you can?"

"Sure," I said — that kind of *not*-sure sureness that directly referred to the fact that I had not been listening to him this entire time. I couldn't even remember her name.

"Thanks, Jupiter," said Vadim, clapping my shoulder as he stood. "I do really appreciate it a lot."

I was about to correct his English, but he was gone.

My classes had finally stabilized. The first day that I left Mr. Denisof's last-period class and realized that I hadn't needed to look at my roster all day, I knew that North Shore had finally sunken into my brain and took root. My classes were going alright, and I'd even managed to get some credible work done. I wasn't part of Vadim's Illuminati or anything, but I didn't need to be. I was finding my place.

Much to my sadness, Ms. Fortinbras stopped subbing in our English class. Our new teacher came in, a paleoanthropic, wheezing hunchback of an old lady named Mrs. Pearltrusser. On the first day, she passed back mothy and yellowed stacks of *Paradise Lost*, collecting the copies of *Ender's Game* that Ms. Fortinbras had offered us. Meanwhile, Mr. Denisof still treated me like an ugly stepsister, calling on me for the hard questions and ignoring me whenever I raised my hand. But I was still managing to tread water.

After school, Vadim helped me with my homework. Then I helped Devin with her homework. I struggled to get downtown as often as I could, hopping through the back door into crowded buses, or walking up to the Broad Street subway and sliding under the turnstile as soon as the fare officers had their backs turned.

And, for the most part, I was successfully managing to avoid Bates.

That day I was feeling, as The Cure said, a two-chord kind of cool. Some guy I didn't know invited me to a party downtown that Friday night, and although I knew I wouldn't be able to go, I thanked him and wrote down all the details — just because information was commerce, and I wanted to feel valuable. I skipped Mr. Denisof's class and, just as I said I would, met Vadim on the nerd steps and let him introduce me around to his new crew. Satisfaction positively oozed from the pressed collar of his pinstriped shirt.

He leaped to the bottom of the stairs, which made it really hard for this to appear casual. "Hey, guys," he said, standing in front of them all, as nervous about speaking to a crowd as a first-year teacher on the first day of school. "I'd like you to meet Jupiter, my best friend. We grew up together in Russia, and then we grew up together here. He — uh — he is really cool, and he knows almost as much about *Doctor Who* as me, and he's never skipped a grade cause he's kind of an underachiever but he's a really cool guy anyway. I, uh, promise." He took a step back.

I don't know if he was waiting for an official proclamation that he was allowed to bring me up on the stairs with him, or for something else, but if he was expecting any sort of impressive, united reaction, he didn't get it. Most of the people there barely looked up from their laptops.

That didn't deter Vadim one bit. He grabbed my arm and pulled me down onto one of the first steps. There was barely any room, and I squeezed myself between Vadim and this distant-looking, pale-skinned girl who he introduced to me as Cynthia Yu. Her eyes flickered away from her laptop for a fraction of a second, barely acknowledging my presence.

Vadim, whose small, Cabbage Patch body hardly fit into the space where he sat as is, grasped his kneecap, trying to pull his legs crossed. He leaned back onto the step above him, stretching out his arms and looking even more gawkward. "Jupiter, this is Cynthia," he said, oblivious to her obliviousness. "She's been really cool, showing me around and making sure that I know where all my classes are and that people talk to me and stuff. Cynthia, this is my friend Jupiter."

I nodded politely to her. She raised an eyebrow and flickered a momentary smile — sympathetic? — my way. I looked at Vadim for help.

Vadim had engrossed himself in the pages of a huge, dusty-looking textbook that sat in the lap of a fat, dusty-looking guy with a white-kid Afro. He stopped pretending to look and leaned over. "Isn't she great?" he hissed in my ear.

I smiled and sank into my stair.

Half an hour later, I'd listened to more snot-coated laughs about math jokes than I'd ever wanted to hear. I was bored out of my skull, and my verdict on Cynthia Yu remained unchanged.

It didn't take a world-renowned specialist in adolescent behavioral psychology to see that she didn't have the hots for Vadim — not to mention the conversational skills, attention span, or social capability for Vadim, either. And I was not a world-renowned specialist in adolescent behavioral psychology.

"So?" Vadim demanded eagerly once we'd left the Tesseract Fan Club. "What do you think, Jupe?"

"I'm really glad you introduced us," I said inoffensively, in my best politician voice.

"Well, yeah, but what do you *think*?" he said with an impatience like the Lord waiting for the right moment to rain down fire and brimstone on Gomorrah.

"Oh, man," I said. "You really want to know?"

Vadim bobbled his head enthusiastically.

"More than anything," he said. "What do you think, Jupiter? Do I have a chance?"

I sighed. I scrunched up my forehead. I thought about how to break it to him easy.

I opened my mouth.

Five minutes later, I was finished.

"Never talk to me again," said Vadim. His face had turned as red as that physics experiment that he'd accidentally blown up the lab with last year, and a similar smell of smoke was coming from his ears.

He gave a huge huff, shoved his heaviest textbook into my stomach, and stormed away from me.

In the first-floor hallway, foot traffic was backed up through the main entrance, four thousand students trying to fit through three narrow sets of double doors. Because of the sudden infusion of bored and sweaty teenagers into the corridor, and because of the humidity in the air, the south doors were wide open, ushering in a half-stale breeze that made the hall almost bearable. I could see straight out to the South Lawn. It was empty today. If the coast was clear, I would have to spend less than two minutes running down the hill on my way to the downtown bus. And it would cut out three blocks of walking.

Was I really going to push my luck?

Of course I was.

I poised on the step, the threshold of the South Lawn. I looked left, looked right. In the distance, Crash Goldberg and his friends were clustered in a circle, madly cheering someone (or something) on.

I tentatively climbed down the steps, walked a few cautious inches onto the Lawn itself. The sun had never shone this bright above Philadelphia, and the street was never so empty. The grass had never looked so green.

I felt a big hand dig into my shoulder. Nails filed sharp, fingers as fat as sausages. Even before I turned around, I could smell breath, hot and salty like raw meat, crusting my ear.

Bates screeched to a halt behind me. His shoes dug into the gravel beneath our feet. A rock flew into my shoe, and when I leaned back into my heel, it dug into a tendon and hurt like mad.

His face had an eager expression on it. I knew what that meant.

I ran.

Branches scratched at my bare arms. Leaves smacked my face. He caught me quick, before I even made it to the curb.

"What do you *want*, Bates?" I said. I don't know what made me so forthright. I knew, or at least strongly suspected, it was going to get me killed. But, in the on-off switch of my brain, I almost didn't care anymore. It was like, we'd come this far, and he'd tortured me this long. I was not going to live like this until the end of high school. Dammit, I had played the system just as well as he had; I had earned my right to be here.

Bates spun me around. I was facing him straight on. The bloodshot eyes, that raw meat smell. I was getting way too familiar with this position.

His face, if still stuck in its omnipresent snarl, felt — if not more comfortable — at least a little bit familiar.

"So, like," he said. "What's your deal?"

Those words, coming from his mouth, sounded so weird. Like alien language, like he was possessed. From Bates, it felt somehow wrong, like they should be growls or curses or a throaty leopard snarl. Did Bates speak that way to his mother? Did Bates even *have* a mother? So many questions were popping up in my head, I didn't even have time to contemplate what I was actually supposed to answer.

"What's my deal?"

"Yeah. What's with you? I see you with the geeks, the preps, the shitsville ghetto kids. When you're in the same shit I am with Mayhew, you get out of it. What's your deal — you been getting it on with Ms. Fortinbras or something?"

"*What?*"

"No offense, man. I'm just askin' — I respect your privacy and all that."

"Well, *no*." I felt a trembling begin in my wrist, work its way up my arm and then back down my spine — actually, I *had* had a few thoughts about Ms. Fortinbras being pretty hot. And when you considered she was a teacher, which you'd think would be something to decrease her hotness, it actually, in my mind, did the total opposite. She was smart and funny and insipid as all hell, and she had a great body, and we totally had to do whatever she said. How had Bates known that about me? Had he been playing some crazy Satanic mind games, burning goats to see into my head?

He peered at me through slanted eyes. "Really?"

"I mean — not that about Ms. Fortinbras, no. Bates, why are you asking me? Is this some mind game where you're going to lull me into a false sense of security and then dislocate my nose or stick jalapeño peppers up my butt or sacrifice me to goats?"

Bates winced at the bit about the jalapeño peppers, but otherwise, he squinted at me like I was speaking in tongues. "Hey, look, man, if you don't want to talk, you can just go," he said. He gestured toward the boulevard that lay before us.

"And you'll just let me?"

"Well, no. I mean, I'll probably give you a black eye or something, but just for aesthetic purposes. I can't just let you walk away empty-handed."

I considered. "Okay . . . so what do you want to talk about?"

Bates waited, as if he hadn't at all expected me to choose that option. When he finally did speak, he did it in a completely different voice — methodical, plotted out, as if he was taking baby steps on the moon.

"I want to go downtown with you," he announced at last.

"What?" I said, and then, "Why?"

"To meet guys," said Bates.

8. SAME DEEP WATER AS YOU

The day was clear, not a cloud in the sky. The outside temperature was exactly the same as the temperature of a warm bowl of soup, and the wind was a tepid massage rubbing at my skin. Bates's face was honest, plaintive. As if his meaning was clear as day and *I* was the one who was being completely obfuscating, instead of the other way round.

I looked at him askew. "You mean, like, other kids to beat up? Or metal guys — like, other guys like you? I've only been down there a few times before, I swear, I don't know where any concerts or anything even *are*."

"No," said Bates matter-of-factly. "Like, guys to date."

I didn't know how I got roped into these things. Most of the problem-child moments in my life, from the time I swallowed all the glue in first-grade arts and crafts class and onward, began the same way — I started taking people seriously and didn't know how to stop.

We climbed on the bus together that day. The driver was my

regular driver, who gave me an even weirder look than usual. I popped in an extra token for Bates. He nodded curtly at the driver, brushed past me, and went straight to the seats in the back where he plopped himself down, taking up the entire row. He sat with his legs spread wide, elbows resting on his knees, hands dangling absently between them. His eyes went straight forward. His nose twitched as if he was sniffing the air for danger. I noticed that he had left his staff back at school. Every few minutes, he would glance over at me, making sure I was still there, that I hadn't wandered off and was still sitting up straight in my seat. When the window views started changing from run-down ghetto neighborhoods to gas stations and warehouses and then to skyscrapers and coffeehouses, his gaze never left me.

"Th-this is downtown," I managed to stutter. "So, whe — uh, just where exactly were you thinking that you wanted to go?"

Bates's lips barely cracked open. In the small division of his mouth, his teeth still gripped each other.

"Just go wherever you usually go," he snarled.

I yanked the stop cord at Twelfth and Vine, one of the places I usually liked to get off. The main downtown action was still a few blocks away, but I liked to walk for a few blocks to get myself out of school mode and into the swing of things. Twelfth and Vine, I figured, was far enough away from the coffeehouses and record stores so I could avoid being publicly embarrassed, but still populated enough so that Bates wouldn't be tempted to dump my body somewhere.

I scampered down the rear steps. Bates was right behind me. The bus deposited us on the corner, a graffiti mural facing us to one side, the early autumn wind blowing at us from the other. I folded my arms, looked one way first and then the other, and scrunched my face up in confusion.

"Do what you'd normally do. Pretend like I'm not even here," Bates instructed.

I gave him one last look of uncertainty. He gave a firm nod. I turned around, looked in the direction of the city, and plotted. The coffeehouse, where we would be seen, inspected, and on display for the entire community of people, was out of the question. So I turned down South Street, into the swarming throng of bizarre-looking locals and European tourists who mobbed the sidewalk, and headed for Repo Records.

From down the street, I could see their sign hanging. Only the interlocking *R*s and part of a vinyl record were visible, the rest obscured by band stickers and concert posters. I don't want to sound too melodramatic, but I got a little chill. In this dangerous jungle of leading Bates around, it was like I'd sighted my backup.

We stopped in front of the door.

Or, rather, Bates stopped me. "No one around here's gay," he hissed in my ear. "Take me somewhere else."

"I don't *know* anywhere else," I insisted.

Bates's grip on my shoulder tightened. "Stop being kvetchy," he said. "Or I'll —"

Heat rushed to my face. Suddenly, I felt all the fear in my body changing to something else. At first I thought it was anger, but then I realized — it was annoyance. Bates might still be bigger than me, and he might still be one step away from beating me into chewing gum, but he wanted something from me. And that meant, one way or another, that I was in control.

"You'll *what*? Look, Bates — I am about ninety-nine percent as clueless as you. This is the only place I've ever seen any kind of gay, lesbian, or otherwise non-heterosexually themed people or propaganda on display in any store, *ever*. I seriously don't know what you're expecting from me, or where else to take you, or what I'm supposed to do to prevent getting a bloody nose by the time this is over. So unless you know where the local underground disco bar is or unless you've got a better idea, this is our first stop. Got it?"

I jammed my hands into my pockets — quickly, because I didn't want him to see how thoroughly my body was shaking. In reality, the only totem of gay culture I'd ever seen here was two guys with crew cuts and leather vests holding hands while they checked out the David Bowie section, but that was the firmest lead I had.

Bates nodded his assent, and we walked into the store.

Today it was mostly empty, the aisles devoid of people, the floor-to-ceiling black, chipping, wooden CD racks looking relatively neat and unscoured. On a busy day, there'd be jewel cases sticking out of the racks, lying overturned on their sides. The clerk, at least, was my favorite one — this absolutely beautiful pale-skinned, long-black-haired goth who wore mercifully little makeup and actually looked less like a goth than a ghost — the ghost of a quiet, thoughtful, and gorgeous porcelain girl who rarely said more than three words in a row to customers, even when ringing up their purchases.

"Where are they?" Bates hissed into my ear.

"*They* who?" I shot back.

"The kids you wanted to show me. The queer kids." Bates said *queer* like he'd been practicing it — like he'd tried out all the words to see which would fit, and this was the one that sounded the least gay.

He brought his face away from my ear for a moment, glanced reflectively at the vinyl section in the back. "Do they have a special aisle where they hang out? Is there something you say to the chick at the desk that lets her know who you're looking for?"

"I really don't think so," I said. I spun around, bent down, and immersed myself in the flyers on a milk crate by the door.

Bates crouched down next to me. His breath blew into my ear. "Go up and ask."

"I can't go up and ask!"

"Just *ask her!*" he hissed.

"I'm not going to just walk up and ask her!" I protested loudly.

"Why not?" Bates held a metal-lined fist to my face.

"Because she's devastatingly beautiful and I have a crush on her!"

That last part, I shouted out, exasperated — which turned out to be way too loud for the fairly tiny record store. The clerk, as well as two twelve-year-olds in the Punk/Post-Punk section and the middle-aged lady with the mullet who was leafing through Foreigner records, all looked up.

My face turned the red of blood and new cars.

Bates flashed the world's widest, most horrifying smile in my face.

Then he pulled back his arm and hit me on the shoulder.

I stumbled. Propelled by his momentum, I lunged forward, practically slamming into the cash register — and into the girl who was working there.

"Need help?" she asked.

She had huge eyes, eyes that looked like a Halloween special effect. They seemed to have two distinct irises, an ordinary blue one with a deeper, purple-black iris inside it.

I could feel my face growing even redder.

This had to be the worst part. Worse than all the other parts of today put together. Blushing was the un-gothiest thing I could think of.

"Actually, yes," I said, leaning into the cash register — close and confidential. "Do you know where the gay clubs near here are?"

She blinked in surprise.

"The gay clubs?" she repeated, as if checking to confirm just how devoted I was to this notion of discovering a club that was convened especially for people of the gay persuasion.

I shot her a little smile back. It felt like my entire face was rolling itself up into a ball, swallowing my eyes and nose and ears down my throat. She leaned back, rubbed her chin with a lace-gloved hand, and watched me fidget. God, of all the possible first real interactions I could have had with her, I think this would rank at just about the number-one worst.

On the other hand, there was always Bates's fist as motivation.

"Yes, those ones," I said. "I mean, it's really okay if you don't, we were just wondering if —"

"ALRIGHT, STORE'S CLOSING EARLY TODAY! PLEASE MAKE YOUR WAY TO THE CHECKOUT COUNTER TO PAY FOR ANY AND ALL PURCHASES, AND IF YOU MONSTERS IN THE BACK THINK I'M NOT GONNA NOTICE YOU TRYIN' TO SNEAK THOSE GREEN DAY CDS DOWN YOUR PANTS, YOU

GOT ANOTHER THING COMIN'!" Her head tilted back, and her mouth opened farther than I'd ever seen a human mouth open. Her hand came down on a call bell on the counter, and instead of a dinky *ding* came a huge reverberation that rang throughout the store.

The woman with the mullet dropped all the records back into the bin but two, and handed those to the clerk, along with thirteen dollars and ninety cents exactly, which she clutched in her hand. The two tweeny boys scampered out right after her, leaving a trail of CDs on the floor in their wake.

Bates craned his head to watch them run away, fascinated. "You want me to run them down for ya?" he offered keenly.

"No, that's fine," said the clerk girl, whose voice returned to its normal autumny whisper, but still felt different, like she'd let go of all the pretense. She stepped over the CDs on the ground, reached into her plaid tartan skirt for a key, and stuck it into the front door. "They didn't swipe anything; I was keeping count. I'll pick up those tomorrow. Besides, are you coming with us — or is your diminutive friend here the only one who's looking for queer kids?"

"No!" Bates roared — and then, embarrassed, coughed into his hand and started speaking at a normal volume. "I mean — I suppose I could be persuaded to accompany you guys. But where the hell are you gonna take us?"

"Just come," she said, walking past us and out the door. Mystified, Bates and I looked at each other. We both felt clueless, all our hunches without base. We'd never before had so much in common.

*   *   *

The club was called Bubbles, and ordinarily — she told us — it was one of those ambiguously gendered clubs for twentysomethings. "You know, eighty percent straight, but they play enough Pet Shop Boys to keep us coming back," she said, laying one soft hand on each of our backs and guiding us through a narrow, black-lit corridor that was lined shoulder-to-shoulder with people leaning against walls that were painted with black and white globs like a cow. "One afternoon a month, all the city's queer youth organizations pool their money together and rent out the club so that the underage kids have a chance to meet each other and get their groove on, too."

We ducked underneath a couple of skinny guys in white tank tops and rainbow necklaces who were making out in a doorway, and stepped into the next room, which was lit in bright orange, glowing neon tables and kids dressed up in the quirky, Day-Glo colors of cartoon characters. Heavy, pulsing thuds of techno music rocked our stomachs. I had to blink. It felt like night in here, like it had instantly gone from four o'clock to ten-thirty. It felt even weirder when I looked at our surroundings: This was an actual club, something I had heard about before but had never seen with my own eyes. People came here and drank alcohol, fancy alcoholic drinks in bright colors with little umbrellas. People came here to flirt with each other. I looked over at the luminescent red vinyl couches, the shiny metal poles. People might have made out right where we were standing. People might have actually had sex in this room.

"Wow, Bates," I said. My head couldn't stop looking around, mouth open, eyes wide. "I guess we found what you were looking for."

"Yeah," Bates echoed back, gazing around the room, his brain in a similar orbit to mine. His voice sounded smaller than ever, as if something had finally managed to make an impression on him. "I guess we did."

"So," I said, picking up a carrot stick off one of the appetizer trays they had lying around, "this is what gay people look like, huh? And this is what they do with their time."

"This is what they *want* to do," Bates corrected me. "They spend the other twenty-nine days of every month waiting for this shit to go down, and as soon as it breaks, they leap on it."

I chewed on my carrot, listening to him speak. It was fresh and crunchy. My teeth sank straight through it. "Yeah, that's pretty much what I was thinking," I said, baffled by his vocabulary, but trying not to let on. "So, I don't know how it works. Are you supposed to notice guys that are cute and start talking to them? Or are they supposed to notice you?"

"I don't *do* 'cute,'" Bates snapped. He caught hold of himself. "I don't like *cute* guys. I mean, I don't frickin' know. I've never done this before. Shit, do you think I'm *supposed* to be somebody's type? Are there secret signals or something?"

"Actually, I'm pretty sure that anyone would notice whether you were their type or not," I said, subtly trying to communicate to Bates how, in a room full of boys wearing designer jeans and sequined sleeveless shirts and girls in vintage polka dot skirts, he was pretty much the only one who fit the two-hundred-pound, leather-wearing construction-worker type. If that even existed for teenage gay kids. Why hadn't Bates kidnapped Sajit instead of me? He was a bona fide gay boy, while I was just an innocent bystander. If there was a secret handshake, Sajit would know it

113

for sure. Maybe that's why Bates would have been nervous about talking to Sajit? It was kind of funny to think of Bates being totally intimidated by Sajit, of all people.

Bates grabbed my arm and pulled me across the room. "Hold on, Jupe," he said, "I want to talk to this guy," he said, grabbing my arm and pulling me across the room. He stopped in front of a clean-cut guy in a team-letter jacket that was the colors of our school.

"Hey," Bates said to him, "don't you go to North Shore?"

"Yeah! Hey, I'm Ryan," he said, extending his hand. "Pretty cool that we're all in the same class, isn't it?"

As a reply, Bates wrapped his hand around the nape of Ryan's collar, pulling his face close to Bates's own. Even from a few feet away, I winced. Ryan was getting the same introduction to Bates's all-day morning breath that I had gotten back in the music store.

"You tell anyone I was here, and I'll rip out your placenta," he growled.

"Uh . . . okay," stammered Ryan.

"Hey, Bates?" I said, cutting in. "Guys don't have a placenta."

"Well then," he glowered, "I'll keep digging till I find it. Ain't that right, sport?" He leered over at Ryan. "After all, *some* of us have secrets to protect, straight boy."

I felt my face redden, felt a sudden, deep embarrassment at having been called out. Meanwhile, Ryan had detached himself from Bates's hand, took one step back, and was shaking out his shoulders. "Harris Bates," he said.

"Wait," growled Bates. And then, "What are you *doing* here?" And then, "So you're . . . ?"

"Well," said Ryan, just as a particularly annoying mid-'90s techno remix came on, "I'm not here for the music."

Bates's face broke out in a toothy, sea-shanty grin. "Alright, man!" He chuckled. "Nice. Don't worry about Jupiter. He's not gonna do anything. I've got him trained. Fuck, he doesn't even *breathe* unless he clears it with me first."

Ryan, not sure whether to take it as a joke or not, assumed the best and laughed, hitting Bates on the arm in that comradely way that jocks always do. I was sure it was going to set Bates off like a cell phone in a gas station.

Bates, though, didn't show any signs of werewolfing out. He didn't even break his smile. "This is frigging crazy," he was saying to Ryan. "Who else is undercover at North Shore? You think Mr. Denisof is gay, since he's always calling different guys in our class pussies? Think he's trying to make up for something?"

I could feel the party rapidly growing more exclusive. Now that I had helped Bates find himself a community, I was back to being the lone alien on my planet. "Hey, take it easy," I said, giving Bates's arm a friendly slap. "I'm gonna take off."

Bates had caught my hand in mid-slap, and now he looked at it like he was going to break it. Then he tilted his head, thought about it, and reconsidered. "Yeah, I'll see you later," he said. "Remember — one word about this and your neck turns to toothpicks."

"No problem," I said, nodding to Ryan and ignoring Bates as best as I could as I took off — straight out the room and down the corridor.

Outside, it was still close to daylight. The afternoon sun hovered over the expressway, reflected over and over again off the hoods of thousands of cars, all frozen in time. With the ghostly, ambient techno of the club in the background, the traffic stand-still seemed almost beautiful. I decided at that moment that I understood people who liked listening to electronic music — it was happy and artificial and instantly nostalgic, the feeling of a party bottled up in a CD, something you would always be able to listen to and remember that moment of connection, of rejoic-ing, that moment when you fit in.

"Hey," came a voice at my side. "Lost your date?"

I turned. It was the clerk from the record store.

"Nah," I said. "He's still downstairs — he's moved on to bigger and better. Not that he was my date in the first place, anyway. We're — uh, just friends." I realized how ludicrous this sounded even before I said it, but I'd said it anyway. "Not like that, I mean. We, um, we're mostly after different things in life."

"Yeah, I kind of picked that up." She joined me in lean-ing against the wall, then followed my gaze out to the sun on the cars.

"About the time I confessed my secret crush on you?" I asked.

"Actually, the first time I looked at the two of you," she said. "The way he looks at people, like he's sizing them up — he's weighing their secrets against his own. He reminds me of my fake boyfriend from high school. He's a textbook example of a closet case. You, on the other hand — well, your shirt and jeans are two different shades of black."

"Yeah, so?" I huffed, indignant.

"Color coordination." She nodded slowly to herself, as if confirming her own theory. "Sorry, but for you to pass as gay — well, you'd need a totally different wardrobe. And let's not even get *started* on your hair."

"What's wrong with my hair?" My hand shot up instinctively.

"Nothing, really," she said, laughing to herself. "Nothing at all."

"That's alright," I said, looking down into the cupped valley of my hands. "I didn't really have a crush on you, anyway."

"It's okay — you don't have to say that. I took it as a compliment."

"No, but I'm feeling honest. I don't know — when I come into the store every day, there's like five different girls at the register, and I developed different stories in my head about you all. What neighborhood you live in. The music you're into. I liked to think that we could talk to each other in songs, and they'd remind you of the same things they'd remind me of. You know that Dead Milkmen album, the imported one you had in the shop until last week?"

"*Metaphysical Graffiti*, that version from Brussels with the five extra songs that they recorded in Flemish?"

"Exactly. So, I've never heard the Dead Milkmen before. I've just looked at their album covers every day for a month, thinking about what the music must sound like. I just have this vision — I just have this idea — that it would fill something inside of me, explain something about the world that I never understood. And that *that*, somehow, is what I'm looking for in a girl. But you know what?"

"What?" She was watching me intently, listening to me for real now.

"It's not. When you started talking to me, even before I knew — not that there's anything wrong with this — that you were gay, I just had this sense that you were someone completely different from the person I imagined you were. And, I mean, you're probably better than that person—you've got a whole life I don't know about that's totally better than the one I made up for you. But my own imagination is why I had a crush on you, and that probably means that what I had a crush on the whole time isn't even you."

I smiled at her apologetically. "I'm really sorry," I said. "I didn't mean to talk to you like that. Actually, it was just kind of rude in the first place. I should probably just stop talking and walk away. I'm sorry."

She had stopped paying attention to the cars completely. Most of the other kids out there had abandoned their cigarettes, were heading back to the city to find a diner, or back down into the club for one last song before the bouncers started shipping out the underage kids. Standing in the cigarette alley suddenly felt naked and private, the type of moment that I shouldn't be sharing with someone unless I really cared about her. Certainly not with someone who wasn't interested in me at all. In That Way, I mean.

She reached over and rubbed my hair.

"Don't worry," she said. "It's cool. You're actually not a bad guy, you know?"

I was about to say thanks, even though I didn't really know what I was thanking her for, when Bates stumbled out the doors of the club, rubbing his eyes from the sun. He ambled over to us.

"Hey," he said. "What are you up to now? You want to get out of here?"

I looked at the record girl. She flashed me a knowing smile, then nodded at both of us. "Go ahead," she said. "Come back some time, though. This happens every month. Now you know. See you around."

She disappeared, and, when I turned around, Bates was already moving away. We set out down Front Street, the buildings framed in the half silhouette of a setting sun.

"I don't know," said Bates. He walked with his hands clasped behind his back, his forehead furrowed in concentration. "It was an overload, I guess. To see that many gay kids in a room — I don't know. I never thought there were that many gay people in the *universe*, you know what I mean? There were hundreds. Maybe there's thousands. Just in Philadelphia alone. Every guy I've ever had a crush on, it wasn't even a question — he didn't like guys anyway, so what could I do? And all of a sudden, I'm in a room surrounded by them."

"So," I asked hopefully, "did you meet anyone?"

He stopped walking. He turned to look at me directly.

"Nah," he said. "They're all a bunch of pansies."

We lay in Rittenhouse Square, on the grass, on opposite sides of a fountain, staring up at the darkening sky.

"I don't know who I figured would show up," Bates told me. "Another metalhead guy. No, you know what? Not even a metalhead. Just some guy with long hair and a pierced septum and a really greasy soul patch. Or a biker dude. A goth, at least."

"You can't force yourself to judge people on surfaces," I said, feeling a rush of inspiration. I wanted to tell him all about the record-store girl, everything that had happened. "On one hand, you're thinking the whole time that just because he listens to the same music as you, you're going to have all this stuff in common, but once you actually start talking, you could find out that he's a totally different person than —"

"Save it," Bates grunted. "I know exactly what you're going to say. I'm not an idiot, you know." He swallowed, a hard, throaty swallow that sounded either like he was about to cry or like he'd just gulped down a small bird. "I didn't want you to fucking show me around the queer youth of Philadelphia because I was looking for some guy to blow. I just wanted to meet other people like me, you know?" he said, and went on before I had a chance to reply. "I just wanted to walk into that room and to have the DJ playing Slayer, or for there to be at least some other guy who wanted to hear a Slayer album. Not even a guy. If there was a speed-metal dyke, shit, I'd probably be even happier." Just thinking of the image put a grin across his face. "I don't want somebody to fuck. I just want someone to say, 'I know the shit you're going through, and I know about it 'cause I'm going through it, too.'"

I opened my mouth, still staring at the sky.

Before anything could come out, Bates cut me off. "*Don't.*"

"Don't what?" I asked, more startled than anything.

"Don't tell me you know what it's like, okay? Don't tell me that you're different too and that you relate and that you understand what I'm going through and all that crap. Just don't."

I said back quietly, almost a whisper, "But I do."

Bates didn't say anything for a while. I turned my head and

stole a glance at him, nervous about breaking the moment. He was still staring down the sky.

"Because I used to be the kid in school everyone shat on, and, the first day at North Shore, you made it official. And then everyone started being friends with me. Not because they actually *liked* me or anything, but because, somehow, I became acceptable. And still, nobody cares about me or hangs out with me one-on-one or wants to hear what I actually have to say. As long as my accent doesn't get out of control and people like Reg and Devin keep saying hi to me, everyone else will too. And there's still no one I can trust, and I still wind up having fantasies about imaginary girls and CD covers."

There was silence on Bates's end.

Then, finally, he looked over at me and said, "You have an accent?"

I walked home from the bus stop — the same route, the same sights, the same thoughts. Bus shelter, radioactive garbage pile, the long empty boulevard, the sleeping wino. Sometimes it felt like a drill. Other times, it felt like meditation.

The walk home was getting a little darker every day, the curse of an Earth that was sinking slowly into autumn. Today I walked the long way, which took me by the warehouse from that fatal first night, the night I learned how to be popular. It started stirring up something in me — that combination of people, the lonely loud synthesizer dance music, the feeling of a night. The best parties always feel nostalgic afterward, like you'll never get the chance to be at that exact same configuration of party again. And I longed to be back there. I played the night in my mind a million times over again, sometimes hooking up with Devin, sometimes running away with Margie, and sometimes with Crash and his gang. I imagined the last few people out there, closing the party down, standing on the sidewalk, holding on to the feeling of the night. Most of them were drunk, but it was a happy drunk. I remembered saying good night to Devin right there on the sidewalk, blown away by the idea that I was actually talking to her, even more blown away that she'd said good-bye to me. Had she really smiled as she said "I'll see you on Monday," like she was glad of that fact? Had she really leaned over to kiss me on the cheek? Had we stood right over there, leaning against the big warehouse door, huddled in conversation, our bodies almost touching, just like that?

I realized that it wasn't just my imagination rehashing. There really were two people standing in front of the party warehouse.

And then, as I got closer, I realized that one of them actually was Devin Murray.

She had already seen me approaching. It was too late to turn around and run — well, this was the Yards, so it wouldn't be entirely unexpected, but I'd feel stupid just the same.

Another few steps and Devin recognized me for sure. "Jupiter!" she cried, waving to me as if there was a chance I'd pass without seeing her. As if we weren't the only three people currently standing on this dwarfingly huge block of abandoned warehouses.

"Hey, Devin," I said wearily, the energy in my body totally zapped from the day. "What are you doing around here?"

As I got closer, the expression on her face changed from surprise to suspicion. "This is Mr. Goldberg. He owns the building.

He's just finishing up totally *over*charging me for the bill for damages from the party," she said, rolling her eyes to me in exasperation like a secret signal between us. She gestured (like a model; like a game-show host) to the stiff-looking, parent-aged gentleman on her left. Then she shot back, barely concealing her misgivings, "What are *you* doing here?"

"I live — I'm coming back — I mean, I'm just going to visit some relatives around here," I finished weakly. It was too late. I was as see-through as one of Devin's mesh-netting shirts.

"Ah, that's impossible," said the building manager. "None of the buildings down that way are zoned for residential use."

"Yeah," I said quickly, "late night at the office," and I hightailed out of there before either of them could say anything else.

9. HOT HOT HOT

When I got to school the next morning, the first thing on my mind was tracking down Devin Murray.

It wasn't hard. People like that usually advertise their presence as a policy. Today, she was doing it in the middle of a squad of girls, telling secrets to each of them in huddled, confidential whispers, then leaning back and speaking to them all. Each of the girls glared at the others, jealous of the attention being paid to them. Crash and his friends clustered around a locker, swapping Erlenmeyer flasks amongst themselves. From time to time, they looked up, noting who was watching. When Crash saw me pass by, he stuck out his hand. I knew what that meant. Without skipping a beat, I extended out my own and met his halfway in a high five.

Devin heard the crack of our hands. She looked up just as I was saying to Crash that I had been to a killer party last night — not exactly the sort of thing to get me on squeaky-clean terms with Devin. And if she didn't hear what I was saying, then she'd probably just think that I was talking about her.

Devin's gaze was followed in quick succession by the combined gazes of all the twelve or so girls that she was talking to.

I felt my face gearing up to blush uncontrollably, my neck already turning red.

"Jupiter, babe." To my surprise, she met me with twinkling eyes and a broad smile. She swept me up with a friendly arm, wrapping it around my waist, pulling me into stride with her.

I flashed her a broad smile back. I liked this whole being-taken-on-a-ride thing.

Devin brought her face close to mine. "Listen, you creep," she said into my ear, so low that only she could hear me, "you're going to stay out of my path for the next four years, and I'm going to let you carry on with your pathetic, miserable, loser existence in peace. If I so much as hear another word in my direction from you after this, I will personally see to it that the entire South Lawn sets your clothes on fire after school for Freshman Day."

I felt my breath slowing to a halt. My legs froze beneath me.

"Wait," I said. We had just rounded the corner, out of sight from her posse. "I don't want to be on your bad side. I came *looking* for you this morning."

"Oh yeah?" she said. "Cracking jokes with Crash, that's what you call looking for me?"

"I really wanted to talk to you. I don't even know where your locker is; the only way I know how to find you is to look around for the mob of throbbing admirers."

She smiled, momentarily self-aware and flattered. "You really came looking for me? What for?" she asked, looking at me with renewed interest. "And do you really think they throb?"

I took a deep breath.

"I wanted to apologize," I said.

She took a step back and nodded. "Go on."

"I'm from the Yards. It's true. And my family really does live a few blocks down from where the party was; we live inside an old warehouse. Well, for a few more weeks we do, anyway. And I really didn't mean to delude anyone. Especially not you. And I didn't mean to betray your trust, or to use you or play you or make you feel like I was being anything less than totally honest. I just didn't want to tell anyone because, well, because it's the Yards."

She cocked an eyebrow at me omnipotently.

"I went to the same middle school as you, to Malcolm X. But I mostly only hung out with the Russian kids there. Well, them and my gaming group. But we were in the same building every day for the past three years, and — seriously — you never even knew I existed."

Devin looked — not confused, but pensive. Calculating. Not like she was figuring out how to get rid of me, but like she was trying to figure out where I fit in the order of things. Trying to figure out whether I was worth keeping around.

"You know, I thought you went to Malcolm X," she said at last. "Seriously, I'm not just saying that. I guess I always figured that you lived in the Northeast villas, the same as everyone else. And not . . ."

"Not in the scumbaggy armpit of the Yards that we all know and love?" I suggested helpfully, trying to keep it in a good humor.

Devin's mouth struggled, trying to decide whether to act pityingly or go along with my joke. Eventually, her mouth broke into a slow, shy grin, which I think meant that I'd passed, and that we were cool again.

"So . . ." I ventured uncertainly. "Are we cool again?"

"Almost," she said. "First thing — never lie to me again."

"You got it," I agreed.

"And, also . . ."

"Yes?"

She smiled at me, that smooth, semi-flirty, make-you-feel-like-your-life's-worth-living beautiful-girl smile that seemed to be Devin's personal trade secret.

And then she said nonchalantly, "Got any idea how to get your hands on a hundred-and-fifty-gallon beer keg?"

"Are you serious?" I stammered.

No, I didn't say that. Her expression made the question rhetorical — and, besides, you didn't say no to Devin Murray. At least, not if you didn't want to cause a rupture in the space-time fabric of North Shore High, and not if you ever wanted her to talk to you again. And especially not if you cared about your reputation.

Since when have I cared about my reputation? I asked myself, and then I answered my own question: *Since I started having one.* So — how to reclaim a six-foot-tall empty aluminum keg in a neighborhood where entire two-ton containers of oil and iron ore frequently ended up missing?

Yeah, sure.

Perfect.

No sweat.

I could do that.

"Sure, perfect. No sweat," I told her. "I can do that."

"Really?" she chirped, and then trilled "cool" as she started to walk away.

Once I was safely out of her attention zone, and her little jean-enclosed hump of a butt began to squiggle away, something that she said suddenly resonated with me. I lunged toward her, reached my hand out, and caught her forearm between my fingers.

She turned around, startled. "Yeah?" she said.

"Sorry," I said, as a sudden panic seized me and, like every dream I'd ever had about school, I was suddenly standing in front of a crowd, without my homework and without a sharpened number-2 pencil, wearing nothing but my tighty-whities. "Just, what did you just say?"

"What's that?"

"What's Freshman Day?"

She gave me a look like antennae had just popped out of my head.

"Freshman Day," said Devin, "is this big thing where all the other three classes gang up on the freshmen. The last bell of the school day rings, the freshmen get out, and the second they leave school property — the moment they walk through those doors — everyone jumps them and starts beating them. Seriously. That's what my cousin said; her boyfriend used to go to North Shore and he *knows*. It's almost like mass hysteria, like one of those riots they used to have like during those Salem Witch things. People just get possessed. They need to get out their frustration, and they get it out on freshmen." She gave me a big, friendly smile. "Or, anyway, that's what everyone's saying. My friends and I are kind of using it as an excuse to cut last period, go to the mall, and max out our parents' charge cards. You wanna come?"

"Freshman Day," Reg told me later before gym, "ain't nothing at all. Just a story they tell new kids to make them wet their pants at night. I don't know anyone who ever got hit by Freshman Day. Except this one junior on the dodgeball squad — but you ask him and he just looks at you like you kicked dirt up on his grave. He has this scar that nobody ever talks about, they just call it 'The Incident' when he's not around. I don't think it's anything important."

"Freshman Day?" said Dr. Mayhew when I stopped him in the hall. "I have no idea what you're talking about. Perhaps it's best to pay more attention to your classes, Jupiter, and give less heed to the murmurings and urban legends circulating among your classmates."

"Freshman Day," said Crash Goldberg, "is the coolest day in the world. Freshman Day means that, if you're a freshman, you get to do anything. Check this — this whole concept of school, the whole notion, relies intrinsically on the stipulation that the students go along with it. If we don't? If we rebel completely and refuse to go to classes? Then there's total chaos. So, the administration, the Powers That Be, let us have our day. That's Freshman Day. They let us do whatever they want on that one day, and the rest of the year, we let them order us around and control us."

"So it's just for the South Lawn?" I asked. "Do you mean, they only get that one day to do what they want, or only the South Lawn kids are allowed to do what they want?"

"Both," answered Crash with a toothy smile. Then, remembering something suddenly, he jumped away from me and dashed madly out from the classroom.

"Freshman Day?" Ms. Fortinbras said, flashing me an indulgent smile from the teacher's desk where she sat. "I think that's what they call it when they need to act out on some poor, ego-filled upstart freshmen and let off some steam. I don't know who the 'they' is, of course — just that random, anonymous *they* that always seems to be lurking in the shadows of high schools. But seriously, Jupe, I wouldn't worry too much about it. You're not the type of guy who makes enemies or gets on anyone's trash list. I'm sure it's nothing to worry about."

"Forget it," said Vadim. "Even if I *did* know what was up with Freshman Day, I wouldn't tell you. Maybe you can ask all your new, cooler friends what to do about Freshman Day. They don't touch us, you know. They stay away from the geeks. Maybe we don't fit into your little scheme of how to get girls and pass classes the easy way and pretend you grew up speaking English and ignore all your old friends."

Then he slipped back into the crowd of geeks and vanished inside. I took a tentative, investigating step toward them. It was met with snarls of intolerance and a cursory, warning glare from a boy in a wheelchair whose fingers curled protectively around his laptop. He gave me a look like he could change my grades, erase my Social Security number, and/or zap my bank account with a flick of his wrist.

Fearing for my electronic identity, I backed away.

* * *

"Freshman Day?" Sajit laughed. "You really believe in that?"

"What's not to believe in?" I asked, startled. Everyone had a different version of what Freshman Day *was*, but it never occurred to me that all these legends might not even be *based* in fact. The one thing about high school I'd learned so far was, there were secrets everywhere. Was it possible for there to even be secrets about things that didn't happen in the first place?

Sajit beckoned me to follow, then led me into the elevator.

The elevator was legendary. All schools were required to have elevators for disabled students to use, but hardly anybody was actually *allowed* to use them. It was rare that anyone had reason to, and it was even rarer than rare that someone filled out all the forms, waited for them to get processed, and scored an elevator pass.

"How'd you get that?" I said, eyeing his green laminated pass in admiration as he slid it out from his wallet, flashed it to the teacher walking past, and pulled me on with him.

"I'm connected," he said, shrugging noncommittally.

The elevator itself was super horrid. It was decorated with months-old announcement sheets and cafeteria menus, and the floor stuck to the soles of my shoes like flypaper. Today it also smelled like puke, but I still felt like royalty when we stepped in.

"So, Jupiter, man," said Sajit, "where've you been? Word on the street is, you're too cool to hang out with your old friends."

"Not all my old friends," I told him, recognizing the tone of his voice — friendly and teasing, rather than jealous and teasing, the way Vadim's had been. "I've just found a new token gay friend to have instead of you."

"Who?"

Suddenly, I realized I was headed toward a severe danger zone — I might not be allowed to tell.

"I can't say," I said. "But it's someone who you'd never guess was —"

"Is it Bates?"

My mouth hung open. "How did you know?"

Sajit pulled the emergency stop button before the doors could open.

"Honey, *please*. I am the ultimate air traffic controller on high of gaydar, thank you very much."

"But he doesn't act —"

"So, dish!" He was past the headline, past the news, and into the clever back-and-forth *Crossfire* dissection of it. "How did you find out? What have you been doing?"

"Well, for one thing," I said, "we went to Bubbles."

"Bubbles?" Sajit groaned. "*Quelle* nightmare, Jupe. These days, I'm all about the sophistication."

"Damn," I said, sinking back against the wall. I felt a wad of months-old gum touch the back of my spine through my T-shirt, and I immediately lifted myself back up. "Sajit, you're crazy. You're totally hooked up. You operate, like, fifteen different lives, and you've totally managed to pretend you've never even *been* to the Yards. How the hell did you do it?"

He pulled his head back, baffled. "What do you mean?"

"What do you mean, what do I mean? I mean, everyone I know from the Yards is either still in the Yards, or we're so wrapped up in trying to *not* look like we're from the Yards that none of us just *deals* with it. None of us are just happy with what we *are*. Vadim is trying so hard to act fluent in C++ that he barely remembers he owns a Mac. Reg doesn't do anything but sports. And me — well, Devin Murray just found out how close I live to the club where her party was, and now I have to try and convince her not to shame and disgrace me in front of the entire school."

"Man," said Sajit at last, "you really don't know much about being in high school, do you?"

"Of course I do, I've been doing everything —"

"Jupiter, listen — you *don't*."

I clamped my mouth shut.

"First of all," Sajit told me, "you need to chill. The world will not shatter the moment that people discover you grew up in the Yards, okay? And, second — you're doing exactly what you're supposed to be doing. Vadim is going in one direction and you're going in another. Just like you and I did. Eventually, you'll get to some sort of crossroads where you run into each other again, and you'll be able to check in with each other and act like nothing happened, because, really, nothing did."

I was speechless.

I really, really was. I didn't know how, in the span of time since last June when eighth grade ended, Sajit had become so wise. But, dammit, I was impressed. I felt like I'd just had a religious experience. Like, now, everything made sense.

"And, about falling for a girl? I wouldn't sweat it, Jupe. Right now, you're working on yourself. She'll come out of the woodwork when the time is right."

"Oh," I said, dazed and overloaded.

Sajit pushed down the emergency stop button and, after a momentary hiccup, the elevator doors popped open. We were on the fourth floor. My class was on the first floor, and I was already late. It didn't matter. I'd just ridden the elevator. How cool was that?

Sajit was holding the door open for me. "Hey, Jupe. You coming?"

I snapped myself out of it. "Uh — yeah, sure. Definitely," I said, hustling out of there. Then, in a flash, I remembered what I'd needed to ask Sajit in the first place. "So," I said, "what do you know about Freshman Day, anyway?"

"Oh, *that*." Sajit rolled his eyes, sounding as bored as if it were a piece of Hollywood gossip two weeks old. "Well, with all your little extracurricular activities, you've got more of an inside scoop on it than I'll ever have. Why don't you just ask Bates?"

"Freshman Day?" Bates barked out a wholehearted, full-bellied, stuffed turkey of a laugh when I found him in the hall. "Don't worry about it, man. Just come find me after school tomorrow on the South Lawn, and we'll chill."

Freshman Day came and went, both sooner and faster than I'd anticipated. I rolled up to school that day with two of the best iced teas I'd ever made, lime and fresh mint and rosemary, poured inside two empty one-fifth-liter bottles of Jim Beam that I'd managed to beg off Mr. Diggory, who was building a whole glass house out of them next to where he usually slept in our back alley. After school, I took both bottles outside to the South Lawn and handed one to Bates. He reached into his own backpack, pulled out two paper bags in a perfectly matching size, and stuck both inside. We clinked glasses, settled into a comfortable resting spot between two of the gigantic stone pillars that layered the south entrance to North Shore, and settled down to watch the fun.

The truth of the matter is, hardly anybody ever gets nailed on Freshman Day who isn't actually *looking* to get nailed. Through the miracle of school gossip, everybody but me knew about Freshman Day days in advance. All the nerds, weaklings, red-haired kids, and other traditional targets of mindless adolescent venom had in mind to be well out of sight way before the final bell of the day rang. They stuffed their backpacks and got on the first bus home at the end of the day.

Bates and I did see some things go down. Most of them were tough-looking freshmen who'd been bumming around the corridor near the South Lawn, virtually waiting for someone of Bates's stature and demeanor to swoop down and grab them. Once they'd been rolled — it was an initiation rite of sorts, as much as anything could be — they started tossing each other down the hill, jumping on top of them. They stuffed each other into trash cans and hammered on them like drums.

It wasn't like anyone was asking for it. It was more that they were looking for an excuse to do all sorts of ridiculous stuff to each other.

The South Lawn, I was finding, wasn't nearly as creepy as everyone made it out to be. I mean, sure, the kids dressed like they were going to a funeral, and not the funeral of anyone you'd ever want to be associated with. Half the time, their conversations were so obfuscating as to be totally unfollowable — I'd think they were talking about an old monster movie, and halfway in I'd realize they were actually talking about a religion. There was one kid, Casey, who was a straight-up Satanist. But he was actually really nice, and he was obsessed with those peanut-butter cheese crackers and always brought extras, since they tasted disgusting but once you smelled one, you were filled with a craving. He would talk for hours about scientific theories from the '50s and was always really amiable, except that occasionally he'd say something about the coming apocalypse and you'd wonder whether he had insider information.

Everything was cool. I mean, as cool as it could be, considering the circumstances — considering that Vadim hated my guts and that my classes sucked and that I still didn't have a girlfriend, that is. As far as the South Lawn went, I wasn't officially a member — I could feel that in their attitudes, in their speech and in the way they looked at me. When someone heard news from their favorite metal band or a new chain-gang joke, I was always the last one to hear. Since I didn't even know most metal bands' names, that was okay with me. Mostly, I was starting to get known as Bates's friend. His sidekick, even. But, in a place where everyone carried jewelry which was frequently mistaken for weaponry, there were worse things to be known for.

I walked down the hall, the picture-perfect poster boy for well-adjusted adolescent cool. And the sea of faces smiling back at me only reinforced the image. I wasn't really *happy*, but I knew I was doing okay. I was counting down the minutes till I could take a bus downtown to the land of unspeakably cool people who still didn't talk to me. But, until that time of day came, I could chill on the South Lawn and make myself feel cool, cooler than cool. With my own brute squad and my own gay best friend — even if nobody knew it but me (and Sajit).

And so I had another place to hang out, another vessel for my after-school activities. Which was just as well, since I was having to go to further and further lengths to avoid my home life.

"Is official," my father announced to me that night. "We are being evacuated."

"Evacuated?" I repeated, not believing what I was hearing. Then the spell-checker in my brain switched on, and I adjusted to compensate for his language. "Oh — you mean about the house. It's evicted, Dad — the word is *evicted*."

Which was not that much better.

My father didn't even bother trying to turn it into a grammar lesson. He cleared off a space on my bed, which was covered with the folded-out liner notes to ten or fifteen different tapes, and sat down to look at me eye to eye. "We have letter from company, must move out by next month."

"Next month?" I said. "That's not too bad. At least we've got a whole month to pack up and move and find another place." Seeing the furrowed Venetian slits of my father's forehead grow even thicker with worry, I asked, "Isn't it?"

"No, Jupiter," he said. "Is not, really. To find new house is long, long work. And how we will afford it — you know, you don't need to hear none of this. You are still too young."

That was a lie, and we both knew it. That insular, us-against-the-world trust that I used to have, when I was five years old and I thought that my father was a superhero, felt like it belonged to a long time ago. I used to think he was the tallest and smartest and most dependable human being ever created, that the traffic lights would always change on his command when he was in the driver's seat. And now . . .

Well, I wasn't five years old anymore.

Now his head looked knobby and weak. The folds in his skin, the ones that I always used to think made him look like a tree-god, mighty and old and created of oak and cedar wood, now made him look sagging and deflated. The perfect smoothness of his cheeks had day-old stubble in an uneven pattern, spiraling down his neck like a rash. If this was one more stage of growing up, well then, I didn't think I was ready for it.

But some things, I guess, happen anyway.

"Tell me about our family," I said suddenly.

My father looked up from the paper in surprise.

"Our family? What you want to know from our family? Your grandfather he did the rabbi for a small congregation in Lithuania, they threw him in jail and chop off his beard. Your grand-grandfather he lived in Sevlusz, husband of very important woman, she come from Vitebsk, in —"

"No! No — I'm sorry, Dad, I didn't mean to say it so loud. It's just, that's not what I want to hear."

He peered at me with thoughtful eyes, incisive eyes, eyes that wanted to see my next move before I made it. For fourteen years, he'd been the wisest person around me, knew my every thought before I thought it. Now, however, I was a teenager. This was new ground for both of us. Now, my mind was moving in all directions, thinking about girls and parties and the kids at school he always warned me about hanging out with. He didn't know what to think of me, and that scared both of us a lot more than either of us would ever acknowledge.

He reached over and touched the left side of my face, his thumb over my temple, his pinky just brushing my chin.

"Your grand-grandfather, he was glazer," he told me. "Very poor boy, but he was very good at his craft. Not glazing, you understand, which is taking very rough mineral, putting shining coating on, making it smooth and shiny. That is how to do glazing, yes. But he is something different — every job he had was new. He was forever always selling himself. He travel, you know. He travel from town to town, always meeting new people who looking for the glazing, always to find customer. He always say, each job is two jobs. The glaze, that is easy part. First is selling yourself to customer, and that is the real job."

He stopped talking and stared out the window, at the night sky.

"Your grand-grandfather, he is dead when I am fourteen," my father said. "I only been working for him in shop two years, not know him well. My father took over glaze shop then, he run for few years. But it was not the same. He always say, he never have what it take." He shifted his weight on the bed from one leg to another. "Maybe it is same for me. Maybe, for this America thing, we not have what it take."

I finally lifted myself up out of my not-quite-looking-at-him position and pulled myself to the edge of the bed, next to him. I looked at his distant face. The short hairs of his beard were prickly and rough, standing straight out at attention. His eyes were small, glasslike beads. I followed his gaze out the window, crusty with dirt, to the dim silhouettes of stars.

"It's not over yet, Dad," I said. I don't remember if I was speaking in Russian or English, but it felt like both. "You're looking at the stars, aren't you? Even if the view is all crappy and stained, you can still see them. We'll get through this one, Dad. One way or another, it's all gonna come together. It's all gonna happen."

Abruptly, he broke his gaze and looked back at me.

"I was not looking at stars, Jupiter. I looking at window. How is it that rest of your room is so dirty, but the window is freshly oiled?"

Uh . . . went my brain, struggling to keep up with the speed of the conversation. It was true: If you wanted to fool your parents, you couldn't just fool them and be done with it. Once you started tricking them, you had to keep tricking them until either they found out or you moved away to college. And I so didn't have the stamina to keep this up for four years.

"Uh . . ." I said.

He stood up and walked over to the window.

"If it is that you are finally to clean your room, I am proud — but Jupiter, I do not think it is that," he was saying. "Jupiter, my son, are you —"

"Dad," I blurted out, "what's the name of the management company that owns the building?"

He froze. You could tell, he'd been thinking about this for a while. Actually, knowing my father, he was spending every free ion of brain space trying to think of a way to keep us in the life to which we had become accustomed, plotting a way to keep us off the street. I felt bad about the diversion, but I'd been needing to ask him that anyway. "You mean the ones who run our factory? Jupiter, you already know name of company we work for —"

"No, not *our* company. You said they wanted to open another factory, but there were none on the market. Who are the people who actually own the building?"

He looked at me askance. "Why you need to know?"

"I just . . . listen, Dad. I have an idea."

He snapped his fingers. "It say on insurance papers downstairs! Follow me, Jupiter. We find out."

Misdirection. The last refuge of the cornered adolescent, needing to hold on to the only secrets he has left, feeling the predator closing in.

But in this case, my parents weren't the predators. As much as they were trying to fight with me, force me to come straight home after school and to share the salacious, embarrassing details of my life with them over dinner, I knew they weren't trying to fight me. This was just the way they worked. It was the only way they knew how to work.

My mother, seeing me and my father working together, was naturally suspicious. "What are you digging for?" she crowed, peering over my father's shoulder, trying to find out what chicanery we were up to, what kind of devilry was making us suddenly team up, and for what purpose. Neither of us answered her. We just kept digging through my father's ironclad long-box files, tossing aside tax forms and receipts from the hardware store until, at last, my father seized upon the needed document and pulled it out. "Hah!" he cried, holding it in the air with both hands. "Is here!"

I reached between his fingers and pulled the document toward me. It was a cc: of a letter sent from the landlords to the company that ran our factory, whose trucks showed up like clockwork to pick up the fruits of our daily labor. I ran my finger from the body of the letter to the top and checked out the company letterhead myself. "'Golden Property Investments,'" I read. "Dad, isn't this the same logo that's on every building in the area? How can they say they have no property?"

My father let go of the paper, deflated. "Is America," he said, his stock answer for why anything didn't work out, "is complicated legal answer. We cannot know what."

I still held on to the fatal letter, scanning it over, looking for clues, for tricks, for anything that would help us.

"Dude," said Bates, "why don't you just go out with Devin Murray?"

We were lying on the grass in the South Lawn, early the next morning. Like my mother said, it wasn't enough that I had to stay at school late every day — now I was getting there an hour earlier than everyone else, trying to squeeze as much out of my out-of-the-house life as I conceivably could. Large patches of the lawn were flattened, one-directional crop circles left over from Freshman Day, where the eponymous freshmen had been rolled down the hill. But off toward the sides and around the bottom, the grass was thick and tall, perfect for camouflage. Standing up, it came up to our waists. Lying down, the thick, savage blades towered over our heads, rendering us a Huckleberry Finn shade of inconspicuous.

"What?" I said, suddenly struck with the belief that Bates was on crack.

"You like her. That information is uncontestable — you fricking bring up her name every time you're talking about anything to do with school. *I'm so goddamn popular, Devin Murray likes me* and *What would Devin Murray think?* and *Does this make me look like Devin Murray?* You're practically her slave already. The only thing that you're missing is the chance to bump uglies. And she'd probably say yes."

"Even if she would — which she wouldn't — what makes you say that?" I asked.

Bates shook his head in despair. "Listen to you, Jupiter. That's the thing about you popular kids. Heads permanently twisted around so you can't see nothing but yourselves. What none of you realizes is, you're all so popular that none of you has time to be normal kids. *Chess nerds* get more play than people like you and Devin Murray. You're all losers."

My natural instinct, to protest being called a loser, was stifled by two very important other impulses: First, that he had said *you popular kids*, implying that, finally, I had reached the level of being recognized as *one* of those people identified as popular. And, second, the realization that Bates, though now we were almost officially at the level of being friends, could still punch my lights out.

And so I restrained myself, holding back the attack dog of my ego. Instead, I asked, "What do you mean?"

"See, the way I figure it is, everyone's like a band. That's your popularity, that's the way you go through life. And you can be a goddamn Spice Girl or something, where everyone in the fucking universe knows who you are, but only for a minute, and you think you're fucking immortal. Then five days later you're old news, and no one's listening to your shit anymore. Or you can be like Slayer. They're not the most talented musicians ever, they ain't composing symphonies or any of that shit, and they don't care about *Total* fucking *Recall Live* or whatever you wanna call that TV shit. They just play good fucking music. And there ain't a lot of us who love them, but damn, the minute Kerry King plays a guitar solo, I fucking know what it means to be in love. And, me being in love, that's all they need."

"Well, yeah. But these Slayer folks — how many people even know who they *are*? They make music, and maybe it's great, but does it pay the bills? Do they have a place to sleep at night?"

Bates sat up, causing a huge bushel of grass to shoot up behind him. He crossed his legs, gave me an evil, wise look, and leered down at me.

"And you think you're doing any better?"

I sank back. He was right. If I didn't figure something out soon, my family was going to be homeless, jobless, and without much more résumé potential than the lead guitarist of Slayer.

Bates returned to his spread-eagle position on the grass.

"I'm sorry, Jupe," he said. "I'm just givin' you shit. Fact of the matter is, you aren't one of them kids. You don't want to go out with Devin Murray any more than I want to get with one of those pasty rave boys. It's just, that's what life gives us. They're the easiest thing to do."

It was then that I remembered to keep track of time. Without thinking, I seized Bates's wrist and pulled it toward me. I checked his watch.

"You do that again, they're gonna be servin' you for lunch on top of iceberg lettuce," Bates grumbled.

But I was already standing up, brushing the grass flakes off my jeans, and wrapping my bag on my shoulder.

"Thanks for the advice," I said quickly. "Seriously. I'll see you soon?"

"Where the hell are you going?" Bates said, curiosity overcoming his natural inclination to threaten and destroy.

"To save my family," I called over my shoulder, already climbing the hill to school.

I showed up in the exact same hallway as before, at the exact same time. Time to put my plan in action. The girls' soccer team was there, clustered around the same locker, their hands poised over their mouths in the same confidential position. The minute I got there, the first late-bell of the day rang. The crowd had just started breaking up.

I pushed my way to the center, and, finding nobody there, I peered down the halls in every direction. Of course, she'd be the first one gone.

There. Almost out of sight, she was almost nothing but a bump of blond hair disappearing down the staircase to the first floor. I took the stairs two at a time. I took the last half dozen in a single leap, lunged forward, and seized her forearm.

Devin turned around, startled. "Jupiter?"

"Hey," I panted, attempting to recover lost gulps of breath. "How did you decide to have your party in the Yards?"

She crinkled her nose. "'Cause it's the *Yards*, gummo. It just made sense. You don't have to worry about your kid sister and her friends crashing, and who's gonna make a noise complaint to the cops?"

"How did you find the warehouse, anyway?"

"Hel*lo*, Jupiter. From your number-one partner in total wackness, Crash Goldberg. His dad owns a bunch of buildings all over the Yards, all the warehouses around there."

"Oh, man," I said. I took a step backward, straight into a row of lockers. Then I sank, cradling my head. My brain was in over-drive, burning up faster than I could think. "Oh, *man*, Devin. This is perfect."

"Why?" said Devin, looking at me with renewed interest. "You think he can help us track down the keg?"

10. THE TOP

"Well, you were right."

Vadim stood in front of me, atop the tallest hill on the South Lawn, at the end of the day. School had been out for hours, and even the drifters had gone home. His head hung perilously low, as though it was going to roll right off his shoulders, and the acoustics of the ground made his voice bounce off dirt and sound even quieter than it normally did.

I didn't move. I braced for a reaction. Was he going to yell at me again? Was he going to threaten to spill one of the secrets of our nerd past to the entire rest of the school?

"What do you mean?" I said—slowly. Carefully.

"I asked out Cynthia Yu. After school last Friday. We were sitting on the steps, with everyone around, and half of them watching us out of the corners of their glasses. I didn't even do it right, probably. I got down on one knee and took her hand and asked her if she wanted to go downtown and hack the wireless servers of all the office buildings together."

"She wasn't into it?" I ventured.

"She didn't even say no," Vadim said. "She laughed at me in front of everyone. In front of all of them."

"Damn."

"Exactly."

I floundered. "But she didn't actually *say* no? Maybe she just thought it was, like, a really cool idea or something, and she was laughing because she thought —"

"She said she didn't *need* me to hack into those corporations — she could do it in her sleep, with her eyes closed. And then she said that she'd turned down people who were more famous than I'd ever be, and that I probably couldn't even *plot* my chances of getting with her as a Heisenberg principle."

"Oh."

"Heisenberg wrote the *uncertainty* principle, Jupiter."

"So that's good, then. Right?"

"Oh, man, Jupiter," said Vadim, clucking his tongue. He sounded somewhere between disapproving and pitying. "You'll never understand."

I hoped he was talking about physics. I was actually wanting pretty desperately to have my heart broken — or at least to meet the kind of girl who would break it for me.

"This is the beginning of our school careers, you know?" I told Vadim, trying to inject an epic quality into the timbre of my voice. "There are six hundred and ninety-two kids in our class. That means there are over *three hundred* girls for you to ask out. And, I mean — hell, they can't *all* say no. You're one girl ahead of me, and that's gotta count for something, right?"

He turned around and looked straight at me for the first time since we'd gotten into this ridiculous non-fight of a fight that neither of us had started; more like we'd just fallen into it. Anyway, he looked me in the eyes, which he almost never did to anyone, and grinned like the day we'd stepped off the plane to America.

"You're right, Jupe," he said. "I really *am* ahead of you, right?"

"Well — I didn't mean —"

"It's okay, dude. It will happen. It'll happen before you know it. You'll see a girl that you'll want to spend more and more time with, and the stories will construct themselves in your head, building it up into a giant crystal palace of what you want to be — and then, sooner or later, it will all come crashing. You shouldn't try to make it happen before you're ready, Jupiter. It's okay, really." He reached up, way up, and rested one hand on my shoulder. It looked slightly awkward, since my shoulder was higher up than his head, but I didn't want to break the moment. "In fact, I should apologize for getting you involved in the first place, Jupiter — for asking you to check her out. I don't know why I didn't realize you're even more clueless than I am."

I stuttered a faulty, broken protest, trying to explain to Vadim that he wasn't wrong, that it *had* made sense for him to ask me. I was his best friend, and I was an incredibly accurate judge of character, and I was still more popular than him — of *course* he should run his crushes by me for verification.

"Don't worry, Jupiter," he said, digging his fingers into my shoulder in what I eventually managed to realize was supposed to be a supportive squeeze. "One day, you'll find a girl of your own to have a crush on. And, that day, I'll be right there to help you through it."

At that moment, I spotted a bunch of guys approaching us from behind Vadim. Thinking they might be a neighborhood gang looking for a couple of nerds with some extra cash in our pockets, I made an executive decision that it was time for us to hustle. "Listen, Vadim —" I said.

"Uh, hey, are you Vadim from the Nerd Stairs?" one of them said. "We've been looking for you."

Vadim, in an instant, had let go of my shoulder, spun around, and jammed his hand into his pocket — probably fishing for his house keys, the way that the latch-key student Protect Yourself program last year in Malcolm X had taught us to do. "Yes, that's me," he answered. "What are you looking for?"

As they stood there and I got a chance to study them, I started spotting telltale signs — analog watches, neatly groomed backpacks, neckties — that made them look decidedly un-ganglike. The tallest of them, a Korean kid with floppy hair and a T-shirt that said $E=mc^2$ in a neon graffiti font, extended his hand in the same way you'd expect the dean of the Mafia to extend his.

"We heard you got rejected by Cynthia Yu," he said. "We have, too. We just wanted to introduce ourselves and extend our congratulations. Way to go. You're official."

"Official?" Vadim said, flashing a big, mystified look in his eyes that was obscured by his thick glasses.

"You bet," said $E=mc^2$. He took Vadim's hand in a squeezing gesture that was half-handshake, half–high five. "Welcome to the club, man. You want to grab a pizza with us at Mario's and translate comic books into American Indian secret codes?"

My cheeks were heating up, my pulse beating faster and faster — half embarrassed at my own exclusion, half feeling the pressure from the rest of my life. I didn't have any time to stand there and be a proud parent.

I had to set my plan in action.

"You sure you know where this place is, Bates?" I said.

I gazed uncertainly out the bus window, taking in the unfamiliar neighborhood outside. I'd driven past it with my parents on our way downtown, just another neighborhood that whizzed by in the car. In a bus, with stops and starts and people from the neighborhood actually climbing on, it took immeasurably longer.

And now we were downtown. Rows and rows of reflective glass buildings passed us by, each one more anonymous than the last. I felt like a customer at a sushi bistro, just waiting for the right avocado-and-cucumber California roll to pop up.

Bates tapped the bus window with his knuckles, which were loaded up with spikes and faux-iron knuckles. The glass clinked. "Dude, relax. Crash's father's building is at 499 Fitzpatrick Street. Right on the corner. It's bigger than the whole goddamn school, so it's gonna be right in front of us. There's no way we can miss it."

"Are you sure?" My head shot around. 500 Fitzpatrick had just passed by with the suddenness and blandness of every other building, swallowed into the anonymous mess of the past. The next block was taken up entirely by one building, and the fact that its numbers were emblazoned across every window on the first floor — *451* — was far from promising.

"Oh, uh, maybe not." Bates thudded the bottom of his fist against the window, this time in frustration. "Shit. You think his

151

dad's secretly poor and runs his business outta the Coffee World on the first floor?"

I took the letterhead out of my pocket. It was crinkled and balled up, but it was still legible. I double-checked the logo — fancy superimposed spirals and thin, elegant capital letters. It said, written out in too-big fancy letters that swirled around each other like multiple coffee spills, *Four Ninety-Nine Fitzpatrick.*

"I don't think so, Bates," I said. "Maybe we should get off the bus and check. I really doubt we could've —"

I looked up just as the bus whizzed past Two Fitzpatrick West, kept going without stopping to let on the passengers who were waiting on the sidewalk, and picked up speed. The next building on our left was 152 Fitzpatrick Street East, and I hit my head on my sleeve, remembering that every street downtown worked like that. That the numbers went down all the way to zero, then started going up again. We hadn't missed it at all.

Bates, amused, shook his head at me. "I thought I was comin' along so I could be yer muscle," he said. "I realize the irony in my saying this, but, dude — all you really need is a girl. Or *someone* to keep yer panties from gettin' all bunched up, anyway."

Without any clear rhyme or reason, the bus stopped at the corner of Fitzpatrick and Fifth, right in front of a huge, decked-out, marble and glass diamond sculpture of an office building: 499 Fitzpatrick, an exact replica of the Emerald City, and home (as the decorative fountain out front advertised) to the Goldberg Property Management Corp.

"You comin', Jupe?" Bates called from the bottom of the bus

steps. He leaned into the double doors, holding them wide open, as the bus driver glared through the rear window angrily and I sat there, staring out the window at the building, gaping.

We took the elevator all the way up to the top floor of the building. All the elevators were made of glass and looked down on a central atrium. My palms started to ache as though there was nothing beneath us. From this high up, it felt like we were surrounded by air.

"Excuse me, sir," said the secretary, hitting a big green button on her telephone. "You have a Mr. — uh, a Jupiter Glazer, and a . . ." She looked up at Bates and blinked at him questioningly.

"Bates," said Bates. He smiled wide, enjoying the sudden fear that being a two-hundred-pound, metal-enhanced high school student hovering over her desk was instilling in her.

". . . and a Mr. Bates here to see you," she finished.

"It's just Bates," said Bates.

She ignored him and tilted her head downward, listening to the voice talking in her ear.

I couldn't believe she was actually calling Mr. Goldberg from like ten feet away. It seemed way too Star Trek to be real— well, it was either that or it was just straight-up pretentious.

Her head shot back up.

"I'm sorry, Mr. Glazer," she said, "but, as I said, Mr. Goldberg has no appointment scheduled with you, and he really can't just —"

She broke off, realizing only one of us was still standing in front of her. A voice called out from the door behind her, which was suddenly open. "Yo, Glazer," Bates yelled over in an out-doors voice. "Am I supposed to do this alone? Get in here and *talk* to this dude."

Without another thought, I stepped into Mr. Goldberg's office.

If the penthouse office suite of 499 Fitzpatrick hadn't been designed with the specific purpose of intimidation in mind, then it was a really fortunate accident. The office was long and narrow, but almost totally unfurnished, except for a small mahogany desk at the far end which sat with a tiny but expensive-looking computer and a single, mammoth, imposing, leather-upholstered chair with claw-edged armrests. The walls were made of glass. Behind the chair was an awe-inspiring view of the city, sky-scrapers jutting out of it like moles ready to be whacked. On the other side of the desk sat two tiny, uncomfortable-looking utili-tarian plastic chairs, not nearly as big and not nearly as posh and plush and executive-suite as the other one.

We decided to stand.

Mr. Goldberg sat in the chair, clicking away on his com-puter, half paying attention to us. He was big, with wide shoulders and beefy arms, a neat black mop of curly hair with a cowlick hairline, and a poker face that looked like it never switched off.

"Well, boys," he said. His face stayed fixed to the computer screen. "What can I do for you?"

I swallowed. Bates looked at me expectantly.

"Well, sir," I began nervously. I cleared my throat and started again. "I'm a friend of your son. Kind of. My family lives in a factory in a building you own, a warehouse on East Diamond Street in the Yards. The company that runs our factory,

TransGlobal, needs to expand. They want to rent another factory from you, but you won't let them. And they still need extra space, which means they have to kick my family out. And I thought, with all those factories in the area that never get any play — that no one ever uses and they just sit there, empty, until the windows get shot out by gangs and stuff — wouldn't it just be a lot easier to lease another factory to TransGlobal, and you'd make more money, and my family wouldn't have to be on the street?"

Mr. Goldberg stopped clicking. He looked up at me thoughtfully. He lowered his wire-rim glasses and tilted his head.

"Nah," he said. "Good pitch, though. Now get out."

I was speechless.

No, actually, I was riled. I was annoyed. I was irate. I was anything *but* speechless. I'd used all my charisma on him, all the tricks I'd learned in finding out how to be social at North Shore, and none of it had worked.

"But, sir," I protested, remembering to call him *sir* and flatter him. "It's a win-win situation. My family really needs a place to live. We're going to be *home*less — doesn't that bother you?"

"Not particularly," he said. "I still got a ton of people in this city who have homes." His hand shot to his computer, and the sound of rapid-fire mouse clicks seemed to be his way of dismissing us.

Bates, from the corner where he was standing, stepped up to Mr. Goldberg's desk. He spread his fingers out. His hand hovered, like an invading UFO, a foot above the blotter. Then he brought it down onto the desk, straight into Mr. Goldberg's laptop, and, in one swift, deft move, swept everything off it.

"I'll pummel you," Bates said nonchalantly.

155

He raised a fist up to the level of his face and cracked his knuckles, one by one.

"No you won't," Mr. Goldberg said. His voice wavered with a growing uneasiness. "That's illegal."

Bates leaned forward, plucked Mr. Goldberg's mouse — one of the only objects to survive his previous assault — right off his desk, and held it up. Then he yanked it up higher. The cord, disconnected, flopped down limply.

"I know," said Bates, smiling.

Mr. Goldberg rolled his chair backward. One hand shot to his phone, slid it off the hook. He cradled the receiver in his hand. With that same hand, he began dialing a number.

"Young man," he said to Bates, "who do you honestly think I am? A man doesn't go into business in that part of town without having associates. Associates who are equipped to deal with all manner of problems. For the more upstanding kinds of problems, as well as the, shall we say, *scraps* that come along with doing business. And, though I would hesitate to call you upstanding, I need to tell you just one thing."

His eyes narrowed.

"My associates make you look like Strawberry fucking Shortcake. And, at this time of day, they aren't too far away from my office." He stopped talking then, and glared at us from his side of the desk. "Do I make myself clear, boys?"

"Fine," replied Bates. "Then I'll do a ritual."

Mr. Goldberg stopped dialing mid-number. *That* had fazed him.

"A what?" he said.

Bates smiled.

"A ritual," he said again, slowly and patiently. He reached

over to the wall, where he'd propped his staff, and picked it up now. He held the staff with both hands, tossed it lightly up and down in his palms for Mr. Goldberg to see.

"Because," he continued, "I mean, *sure*, you could bring your hired goons down on me. And then I would probably call up my boys, and shit would go down, and your guys would probably win. But — and I want you to know, Mr. Goldberg, that this is not a threat — I would really hate to think of what would happen then. I would hate to wake up in *my* sleep every night in a cold sweat, wondering whether all the limbs of my body had suddenly detached, or if my children's souls were being snatched from their bodies. I would hate to think twice about opening my refrigerator any time I wanted something to eat, wondering whether maggots and house flies were going to crawl out of my lunch meat. I really don't know if I could bear that much *thinking*, Mr. Goldberg. I'm kinda a paranoid person by nature. I'm always . . . worried . . . that something's going to jump out and get me." He pronounced each word slower and slower, quieter and quieter. By the end his voice had sunk to a whisper, and I realized at that moment that listening to Bates speak in a whisper was a lot more frightening than hearing him speak in a roar.

The door shot open.

Crash walked in, seemingly oblivious to the rest of the world. He walked right past Bates and his extended staff; past his father, who held the phone as far away from himself as he could possibly get it, ready to toss it aside the moment a slug crawled out of the receiver. He crossed to the far end of the room, lowered himself down to the carpet, reached into the micro-fridge that sat there, and pulled out a crisp, cold can of orange soda. He stood up, cracked it open, kicked the fridge shut with his heel, and looked up at us. I think that was the first realization he had that we were all in his father's office.

"Oh, hi, Bates! Hey, Jupiter. What are you guys doing here?"

My throat was sticky and dry. I couldn't speak. Bates, too, was too intent on appearing fearsome and Satanic to reply. At last, Mr. Goldberg was the one who spoke. His voice sounded strange and high-pitched, as though he were half expecting to be demonically possessed himself.

"These — these boys were just trying to convince me to sell that warehouse on East Diamond," he said.

"Huh," said Crash thoughtfully, taking a long swig. "Well, I know you were gambling on the Yards to turn into the next big development zone when you bought it, but housing prices haven't gone up there in thirty years, and all the kids at school with rich parents are moving to all those East Liberty developments down by Penn's Landing. I hate to tell you this, but there's nothing going on around there. It's total crap. You really think it's worth holding on to?"

"No," Mr. Goldberg's voice wobbled, "I guess not."

After that, we removed ourselves from the premises of 499 Fitzpatrick as quickly as possible, and stepped out into a surprisingly cold night. I grabbed the end seams of my three-quarter-length sleeves and tried to stretch them into full-length sleeves. It didn't really work.

"Damn." Bates shivered, running his leather-braceleted wrists over his bare arms. "We need to move. Where you headed?"

I was about to reply automatically, *back home*, but something in my brain clicked and I realized, with the dim setting sun, that it had just officially become Friday night.

"I don't know," I said. "There's this party in Fishtown with a bunch of North Shore kids. But I saw this concert flyer in the record store, and I really wanted to—"

I felt Bates's hands grip my neck, a friendly but firm directing power.

"Show me the concert," he said.

We waited in line outside the TLA alongside a bunch of other kids, most of them at least five years older than we were. Someone was holding up the box office, arguing about paying with a charge card. I could feel Bates's frustration bubbling up, ready to manifest itself all over me.

"This band better not suck," he growled. "What are they?"

"I don't know," I replied. "I'm sure you'll like them — they didn't look like they were folk-rock or anything. . . ."

"I wonder how late the party goes. I wonder if there's any freshmen there," Bates mused, his voice held a bizarre combination of wistfulness and bloodlust. "Cause this better not suck."

"Hey!" boomed Crash Goldberg, coming between us, grabbing both our shoulders and shaking us. "What's up? What's going on? You guys into the band? Or are you just here for the scene?"

"What scene?" grumbled Bates, his voice the usual shade of pissed-off, but I knew what he was really asking.

Crash looked around and shrugged. "The kids," he said nonchalantly, nodding at a crowd of people who were all at least ten years older than us. Then he stepped up to the ticket window, laid down some money, and, once he had his ticket, stepped aside.

I opened my wallet. There was a single five-dollar bill inside, all that remained of what my parents used to pay me for working after school at the factory. I took a deep breath, imagined myself standing on the edge of a cliff, and handed it over.

"Wow," I said. "I can't believe I'm investing the last of my cash on a single night out, based solely on a cool-looking flyer."

I didn't say it to score a sympathetic look, but from Crash and Bates's expressions of astonishment, you'd think they were my two biggest patrons.

"Why don't you ask your parents for more?" said Crash. I noticed that he'd paid with a twenty, and stuffed the extra money straight into his pocket instead of putting it back into his wallet.

I fumbled with an answer. Bates jumped to my rescue — not with the answer I would have given, but with the truth.

"He can't, 'cause Jupiter used to work for his parents and then he quit and they hold it against him cause they live in the Yards and they're probably as broke as your finger is gonna be if you ask him any more about it."

From Crash's response to this — an easy grin and a double-backflip-cartwheel while standing in place — I deduced that, though Bates's answer might have sounded like a threat to the casual observer (that is, to me), it was actually just how Bates answered questions.

Fortunately, the box office printer chose that moment to spit my ticket out, and the cashier, a conventional alterna-girl who was watching us with a mixture of confusion and distaste, pushed it through the glass window toward me.

I grabbed the ticket tightly in my palm and ran through the door. After a beat, Crash and Bates followed me into the dark portal of the Prowler show.

"Damn, Crash," I said, hustling into the crowd. "I really have to thank you. You don't even know how much this —"

"Well, don't tell me, then," he said, cutting me off. "Spreading chaos and disorder through the universe, that's my mission. If it helped your state of mind, I assure you it's entirely coincidental."

I stopped talking, not sure if I'd just been insulted. Crash threw his arm around me. His eyes never left the stage, where the band was just walking on.

I opened my mouth.

"Don't ask questions," he said. "Just embrace the chaos. Treasure it. Love it. Stroke it like a pet rhinoceros and make it your own."

I looked at Crash, who was grinning crazily, swaying back and forth in anticipation of the music. No residual thoughts of saving my house remained — no thoughts of the afternoon at all, probably. Crash had the most disconnected, stream-of-consciousness mind in the world. As soon as something new interested him, he threw the old idea out the window of the moving car of his brain and never looked back.

"Hey," I said to him, "at least let me buy you a drink. A soda or something."

"How?" he said. "You got any money?"

"Well," I fumbled, "it doesn't have to be today. I'll owe you."

"You don't need to."

"I know," I said. "I want to."

161

"Okay," said Crash, the corners of his mouth spiraling deeper into that crazy, unhinged grin that, for the first time, seemed to indicate that he recognized me on some level as a kindred spirit. "You're on."

And he pricked a cool fifty out of his wallet, held it up in the air, and disappeared, making his way into the packed crowd in the direction of the bar.

The concert, in and of itself, was amazing. You know how sometimes you can go to a concert and it's just a party in disguise, where the audience is the real act, and other times your eyes never leave the stage and it's like a big great dramatic performance? Well, this was both. The band, Prowler, were like music geeks who'd been hypnotized into thinking they were a Motown rhythm and blues soul-rock band from the '60s. They were skinny white kids in loose-fitting jeans who tinkered with computers in the corner to make a beat, then whipped up their guitars and basses and started laying down a fat, grooving funk track over it. They got down like Prince and James Brown and Christopher Walken all at once. They jumped all over the stage, skidding on the floor, crashing into the amps. They pogoed to their own beats. The lead singer ripped his shirt off and tossed it to the crowd and promised the audience that, if any girl wanted to rip his shirt off, he'd go and find it and put it back on for her.

We danced. Crash was his usual Gumby self, hopping and twisting and somersaulting through the crowd. He picked girls' hands out of the air like they were apples and it was the first day of the harvest, twirling the girls around like trees on wheels. How did he make friends — or crushes — so quickly? I resolved to keep following him around until I figured it out.

Even Bates was having fun, moshing up against guys who were every inch as big as he was, throwing their bodies around and then having them throw around his body. At first I thought it was totally sly of him, getting a sexual charge out of it when none of the other guys would even realize it, and then, in the middle of working up my own dance-crazed sweat, I realized that it wasn't sexual for him. It was pre-sexual, the charge of adrenaline and energy and our carnivorous nature. It was the thrill of dancing itself.

I threw my body into the tantrum of the music, felt it wrestling with my protesting muscles, twisting my feet and forcing my hips out of their sockets. I shook my arms and I shook my head and I shook my long, curly hair, each thick strand dancing with its own cadence and groove. The most beautiful girl in the world, her hair a tapestry of black that glowed like stars under the lights, flowing behind her, danced up to me and, facing away from the stage, facing me, waved her hands in slow motion between our faces, spiraling them like an Arabian princess would. It took me a minute to realize she was the girl from the record store.

She swayed back and forth in a slow, boatlike rhythm, undulating like a Hasidic Jew lost in prayer. For a single, beatific second, she made eye contact with me, moved in, and wrapped her arms around my neck. She smiled at me — comradely, vigilant — like we were the first two people in the world to have discovered this band, Prowler, like *really* discovered them, and this moment was the moment that our true ultimate secret was being bequeathed to the world.

The next thing I knew, she was on the other side of the dance floor, kicking it up with a bunch of girls, one of which I knew was probably her girlfriend. And the others were probably all gay, too, girls who shared her life experiences, of being different than everyone around you, of hiding the world's biggest secret in your chest and of being afraid to tell anyone.

I knew, too, that on some level, I had more in common with her than any of those girls. And at the same time, she had those girls siphoned off to a corner of her thoughts that I would never have access to, where she would never even deign to think of me.

But right then I didn't care. It didn't bother me that she would never have a crush on me, that she would never feel about me the way I felt about her, and that in all likelihood she'd never truly realize the way I felt about her or the thoughts I was thinking or the fact that she'd probably never get to see inside my head, to have that real and true exchange of thoughts that never stopped that I utterly, desperately wanted to share with a girl.

Right then, I was dancing. And I was smiling. And I was perfectly fine to stay in that moment and not move at all, not to wish for anything else.

I felt like the total opposite of a loser. I didn't care what I was doing or who was around to watch me. I just wanted to be exactly where I was, doing exactly what I was doing.

11. JUST LIKE HEAVEN

"Oh, man," I said, my head going wild on a sugar buzz. "I have no idea how I'm gonna get home. Can I just tell you guys, it's eleven o'clock and my parents have probably already issued a police bulletin on my ass?"

Bates lay sprawled out on the concrete outside the theater. Both his face and his massive, solid stomach stared up at the sky. His lungs rose and fell like the tide, taking in deep, unrestrained breaths to replace all the air he'd lost in the pit.

"Relax," he said. "I'm going back to the Northeast, too. The El runs till midnight. We'll take it to the end of the line, and we can split a cab from there."

"Yeah, right," I said. "With whose inheritance?"

"With mine," said Bates, sounding more distant and on-his-own-planet than ever. "Don't worry about it. Just luxuriate for a minute with me, Jupiter. Live in the moment."

I took another glance down at him on the ground, lying there and making time with the cobblestones. Crash stood around the corner, trying to bum cigarettes off of straight-edge kids who kept threatening to beat him up for asking. *Live in the moment.* One day I really would be able to do that. For now, though, I had to content myself with the first step: channeling my neuroticism into watching the only person in the world who really mattered — who was two hundred pounds and frequently threatened to pound me into a pancake and top me with blueberry syrup — as he lay drunkenly on the sidewalk, swinging his fists at the stars.

Behind us, hordes of people poured out of the concert hall doors, singing the lyrics to the band's final encore. A few of them stopped to gape at Bates, earning little more than the shake of a fist in their direction and a warning grimace. "Did he have anything to drink?" I whispered in Crash's ear.

Crash shook his head. "Nada, man," he whispered back. "I swear, sometimes I think that, compared to him, I'm almost normal."

Almost normal. Succumbing to a sudden realization, I wondered if this was the first time I'd ever heard the word *normal* used pejoratively. Growing up in the Yards, normal had never been a bad thing. I wished I could talk normal, act normal, be normal. Even at that fateful first party, I'd spent the whole night wishing I could fit in, and holding my breath out of fear that I didn't. Now I was standing downtown with the star of that party, watching our mutual acquaintance attract the attention of a whole crowd of onlookers.

Suddenly, Bates stopped muttering under his breath. He jumped up, right onto his feet, and started walking away.

"What the hell are you waiting for?" he called over his shoulder. "You want me to take you home or not?"

* * *

At the subway, Bates slipped two coins in, one for him and one for me. Crash ducked under the turnstile when no one was looking. They both lived in East Falls, on the other side of the city, but Crash said they'd ride the El to the end of the line with me and then get on the last subway of the night back in the other direction. Neither of us knew what to say, but neither of us felt like ending the night quite yet. Two stories below Market Street, we could still hear thudding, thumping trance music coming from the clubs above us.

A couple sat on a bench in the station, making out with a passion and furiousness that blocked out the rest of the world for them. Crash stood right next to them and watched. Two old women with grocery carts were talking in Russian. Bates elbowed me and I translated. I said they were listing the narcotics they'd bought and where they were going to sell them.

The train didn't take long in coming. We got on a few cars down from the old ladies. The couple didn't even notice that the train had showed at all, and Crash barely did. He raced across the platform just as the doors were closing, got his left foot caught in the door, and yanked it out just as the conductor was yelling at him over the speaker system.

"Yaaaargh," moaned Crash, nestling his bruised ankle as he writhed on the floor.

"Friggin' klutz," said Bates as he swung into his own seat.

The train was empty. There was no sound but the grinding of wheels on tracks and the whir of the air-conditioning. It felt way too late in the year for air-conditioning to exist. I took the seat behind Bates. Each seat was big enough to hold two people, but Bates had his feet up. I slid into the seat behind him, pulling my feet onto the cushion in the other direction, so I could face him.

"Hey, Bates," I said. "Why were you acting like that before?"

"What?" he said. "You mean, on the ground?"

"Yeah. Were you stoned?"

He looked at me askew. I'd never been a drug user. I didn't know what being stoned was like. It seemed like it must be like that — acting like you're in a totally different universe. I imagined that was what the café hipster kids must do — all get stoned together and lock themselves in a room all night.

"Jupiter. Do you even know what being stoned *is*?"

I gulped.

"Yeah — uh — sure," I admitted, measuring the volume of my voice to sound casual. "It's when you smoke too much marijuana."

He burst out laughing. He laughed like coughing, as though all the phlegm in his throat was going to congeal and coalesce.

"What's wrong?" I asked, stricken. "Isn't that what it is?"

"Yeah," he answered, rubbing his chest and coming down. "No, Jupe, I was not stoned. I was just, I dunno. What my shrink would call *acting out*."

"Your shrink?" Was Bates really psycho? Had he ever been institutionalized?

"She's just this lady my parents send me to. A *socialization therapist* or whatever. They get freaked out whenever I open my mouth, and every few months they need reassurance that I'm not going insane or some shit. So they send me there, and she interviews me for an hour and tells them that I'm fine. I don't know what she would make of *that* monkey over there."

He shot his thumb over his shoulder, gesturing to where Crash was now hanging upside down from the bars on the ceiling, from the very foot that he'd just been moaning on the floor about and threatening to sue the city for a new leg.

"Oh. Right." I was speechless, having nothing in my own life to compare this to. The closest I'd ever gotten to therapy was being sent to my room and then crawling out onto the roof to stare at the stars. Maybe my parents weren't so screwed up, I decided.

"Yeah, well, anyway, it's fun. You get to tell her whatever you want and she has to take you seriously. I make up a new disease every time I come in. She keeps thinking that I'm gay, but I think she's supposed to say that about everyone." He let out a loud guffaw — mostly, I think, for the benefit of Crash, who I'm sure didn't know anything close to the truth. I looked over at him, but Crash had left his perch on the handlebars and emerged in the seat directly behind me. His head popped up like a weasel.

"What are you guys talking about?" he shrilled. "Is it fun? Is it about me?"

"We were just saying what a massive ego you have," said Bates, totally unexpectedly.

"Well, you know, it's actually a learned talent. I mean, you can't just go into the business of being me and expect people to start loving you for the person you are without a little free advertising. It never hurts to get your name out —" he said, smoothly and smartly.

And then he suddenly stopped talking because someone had, at that moment, shoved a knife in his face.

The knife was as long as my forearm. It was shiny and clean, and seemed a glowing, lightsaber white as it reflected the

169

subway car's fluorescent lights. It waved in the air, pointed vaguely at Bates's face, the tip of the blade hovering this way and that with an air of easy threat, as if at any moment it could decide of its own accord to burrow itself in his neck, or to change course and fly out at one of us.

At this point, both Bates and Crash were facing out. I was facing them, which meant I was sitting with my face toward the window. We had just ridden past the Ben Franklin Bridge, a brilliant shade of aqua blue, standing out against the harsh grays and slates of the Philadelphia skyline. The Delaware River flowed quietly, meditatively, dotted with a million tiny glowing waves and lights that reflected the city skyscape.

The knife, too, reflected the brightly glowing lights of the subway car. Only, those were fluorescent and dirty and cold.

And I could see Crash's face in its dull steel, and he looked like I'd never seen him before, like a totally different person.

He looked scared shitless.

"Come on!" roared the guy who was brandishing the knife. "Give us your wallets!"

Us? I thought. I felt my blood racing, my heart hammering in my rib cage, my veins beating against my outer layer of skin. An instant, viscous layer of sweat burst out, soaking my shirt in seconds. I listened intently, terrified. I glanced at the reflection of the muggers in the train window. There was a whole gang of them, too many to count. Five? Six? Eight? They were talking too loud. My head was spinning too fast.

Bates stirred in his seat, fidgeting. I wasn't sure where this fell in the spectrum of his fierce and antisocial urges — whether he was going to spaz out and go crazy or whether he'd be so freaked out by someone who *wasn't* him bullying him that he'd back down instantly. A small part of me, totally scared and totally tailspinning, was hoping that he would start to rage like a mountain lion, hulking out and throwing his fists everywhere, attacking everyone and everything. An out-of-control Bates was still better than an in-control crazy, screwed-up Yards gang with weapons. Not by much. But better nonetheless.

Bates made his move.

Snarling and glowering, he rose to his feet. "Listen up, you mammalians," he growled. "You wanna talk to me like that, you best be talking out of your mouth and not some other — "

"You gonna argue with this?" the main guy said, thrusting the knife closer to Bates. Now it was right up against him. The blade dug into the fatty fold of skin between his neck and chin. It pressed the skin neatly back, straining it, bisecting it in an even crease. Soon it would start cutting in.

Bates's eyes swam with determination. The other guy's friends stared at him. Everyone had thought it would be a simple game, their wills against ours. I don't think either of them expected to have their bluff called.

Then came an explosion from the mouths of one of the other guys in the gang.

"Don't!"

He jumped for them both. He seized the hand of the guy with the knife at the same time as he grabbed Bates's forearm. I don't think he knew what he was doing. I mean, I don't think *anyone* knew what they were doing, but this was a particularly advanced degree of stupid — like plunging into a dark room when you're in a mad scientist's house and there's one of those biohazard signs on the door.

But sometimes, you just gotta throw yourself into it.

Bates tumbled backward over the seat. The guy with the knife soared through the air, flying into the rest of his gang, literally bowling half of them over so they were arranged on the floor in various positions of Twister-like complexity. Bates, meanwhile, was clutching the top of the seat with both arms, holding on for life in a position that, in different circumstances, would have been doing serious damage to his ego. His legs hung upside down in the air. His arms were sprawled out, clutching the pillowy plastic fabric, feet jammed in my face. I don't know how he managed to roll into that position, but there he was.

It was a precarious balance. Too precarious. The visual absurdity of Bates's massive body hanging upside down by a thread, just the utter weirdness that our assailant was lying in the main aisle of a deserted subway car racing across the city, was enough to freeze us all.

And then Bates collapsed.

He fell right into me. Or *onto* me, I should say. I fell on the floor, Bates rolled on top of me, and off of me, and then straight into the gang guys.

In a flash, the members of the gang scrambled to their feet. Two of them grabbed Bates by his arms and held him tightly, like a convict going to the guillotine. They forced him down, brought him to his feet. I backed up against the wall, feeling even more afraid, and even more conspicuous than before.

And then, in the silence that followed, as I trembled and the gang members panted and everyone wondered whether the leader of the pack, the wild one, was really going to use that knife, there came a single, cogent, bewildered exclamation.

"What the hell are *you* doing here?"

I blinked.

I started, actually recognizing the voice before the face. She was just standing there, mixed in with the rest of the gang — short, stocky, bleach-blond pixie haircut, boobs jutting out like they meant business, hands on hips, out of uniform, looking more than anything like she was *pissed off.*

"Yo, hey, what's up Margie?" I said quickly, the words tumbling out of my mouth with a fear that bordered on religiousness. "What are you doing here?"

"Dude, this is what we *do* at night," she said. "You live in the Yards, you know what goes on. This is my man. His name's Jimmy."

At that moment, none of that information was entering my brain. I was only barely aware that she was even speaking. I nodded to Jimmy severely, maturely. "Nice to meet you," I said.

Jimmy, baffled, offered a wave of his hand.

"Hey."

"What the hell's your name, anyway, kid? I keep running into you, but we never get around to —"

"It's Jupiter," I said quickly, answering her while actually cutting off the end of her question. It wasn't really a question, anyway, though. It was somewhere between small talk and getting the particulars of our meeting out of the way.

"For real?" she said, still staring at me like I was a phantasm that she didn't quite believe in. "Well, whatever. Cool. Your parents name you that?"

My mouth came open, about to reply. But she pre-empted me, asking instead, "So what are you doing here? And why are you hanging out with these clowns?"

I glanced around, at Bates and the still-hiding Crash Goldberg, who was currently being surrounded by three gutter punks in gold jewelry and puffy Eagles jackets, each of whom looked more eager than the others to make an imprint of that jewelry in Crash's skull.

I paused. I was on the precipice of telling her everything that had happened since the first conversation we'd had, the first time that I'd met her, in the restaurant. I wanted to tell her about becoming popular, about losing my accent, about hanging out with Devin, and, most of all, about discovering downtown. How there was a world beyond the Yards, and how there were people around that were so cool and how we didn't have to hang out with guys like this, the type of guys who beat me up every day for the first seven years of my public education, the type of guys who probably ridiculed her every time she used correct grammar or spoke in an accent that they didn't understand.

And so I did.

"We're on our way home from a rock show," I said. "It was this band called Prowler. They're amazing. They aren't big yet, they're just a bunch of café kids who leave flyers lying around downtown, but they're going to be huge. They really could do it. And it's amazing — there are all these coffeehouses and art galleries and even some clubs, and all kinds of people hang out there —" I thought about telling her about Bates's and my adventures at Bubbles, but decided now was probably not the proper time. "And it's really completely amazing. And since we talked that first time, things have gotten really insane. I got popular. Everyone at school knows who I am, and I get invited to parties constantly, and Bates even says that this girl, Devin Murray, the hottest girl in school — she's, like, practically the dictionary definition of conventionally beautiful — and Bates keeps saying that we should, like, get together, and I even think he might be right. But you know what? I don't really care. Not to sound arrogant or anything, but I'm not interested in her. She's nice, and she's cool and smart and funny — she isn't any of the stereotypes — but it's just that I'm not into her. Or any of the girls downtown. They're interesting and thoughtful and cultured, they're everything that I wanted to get out of the Yards to get away from, but they still live in their narrow little worlds, afraid to talk to me. They aren't like you at all. And I really think — I keep hoping that I'll run into you so I can tell you — I just want you to know, I think you're really amazing."

Everyone on the train was silent. Bates, Crash, the guy with the knife. The guys who had been looming over Crash, about to capture him or something, actually took a step back. They all waited, curious and uncertain. Everyone looked like they really wanted to hear what was going to happen next.

Then, into the aura of solemnity that I had somehow imposed, someone's voice broke out. It was the guy with the knife.

"Can we *please* get our shit together here, folks?" he bellowed. "I believe we were in the middle of something?"

Margie raised her hand — palm up, fingers stiff together. "Cut it, Jimmy," she said. "Just get off the train or something, okay? We're in the middle of something."

Jimmy looked like he was going to argue with her, but the train pulled to a stop just then. The guys who were holding Bates let go of him. Jimmy sheathed his knife quickly, and they all poured out of the subway car.

And then it was just the two of us.

Margie stood in the aisle, and so did I. We faced each other, suddenly feeling very formal, somehow *meaningful*, as though we were destined to be standing right here, right now. She looked totally different, standing alone in the middle of the car. Her black Guns N' Roses ripped-sleeves T-shirt and cut-off jeans turned her into some sort of postmodern artsy Gothic girl. Her pale skin and even whiter hair made her surreal, luminescent, so vividly and throbbingly *alive* against the dullness of the subway car. Okay, we weren't really alone — Bates and Crash were both sitting on the edges of seats, eyes wide and breath racing, both trying to figure out what had just happened — but, as far as we were concerned, they were in another universe.

Or, at least, as far as one of us was concerned.

"Wow, Margie," I said. "I can't believe I ran into you again. It was really cool of you to save our lives like that."

When I called her Margie, her face scrunched into a question mark, but then softened into an expression of grace and understanding. She laughed a little, candid and sort of nervous. "Hey, no problem, Jupiter. Anything I can do."

"So you'll go out with me, then?" I blurted out.

At once, I realized the severity of my words. I had never asked a girl out before, and I guess I'd always just assumed that it was something that one might bring up naturally in a conversation, along the lines of *How are you?* or *Have you heard the new Cookie Jar record?* As soon as I'd said it, however, I realized the inflexibility of such a question. Like the turning point in our relationship. Like the turning point in my life, and the two vast, extreme directions it could go from here.

"Oh, Jupiter," she said, sweetly and gently. "No."

"Oh."

My *oh* could not have been more different than hers. Margie's was kind, lilting, easy, and noncommittal, the kind of *oh* that is sung more than said. Mine was like a winter blizzard, sudden and hard, a punch in the stomach. Deflated.

"Jupiter, you *met* Jimmy. He's my boyfriend. Granted, he's not very sociable, but what do ya want? He's actually a pretty good guy. Give or take the occasional knife fight. And he's a vegetarian."

I'm a vegetarian, too, I thought about saying, but didn't, because I wasn't.

"Listen, I have to go. I'll grab a taxi at the next stop, hook up with the guys. This is — this isn't what we ordinarily do. They don't even really need money — they have like a *zillion* hook-ups. It's just a thing. It just keeps them busy."

"Uh . . . right," I said, floundering for something to say that didn't sound incredibly juvenile in response to that.

"But . . . you glad I could get you out of that?"

I grinned. "Yeah, just as they were about to puncture Bates like a big red balloon. That part was cool. Thanks for the rescue, Margie."

"Hey, no problem." Like clockwork, the train glided to a stop and the doors slid open. She stepped into the doorway, one (long, thin, ivorylike) hand over the door. She flashed me a smile, which didn't feel charitable so much as purely beautiful, a smile I would have bathed in the memory of for the rest of my life. "I'll see you around, Jupiter."

"Wait!" I cried suddenly. The train was whirring up; the door was going to shut in a minute.

"Yeah?"

"You know that keg you guys stole from the party I saw you at? The warehouse one?"

"Yeah, I remember. It's still around. Marcus has it in his room with a Flyers flag on top of it. Why?"

A computer voice on the subway loudspeakers said, "*Please* stand away from the doors." The standard alarm bells started to go off, and all the doors except for hers slid halfway shut and open again.

"You think I could get it back? There's this girl I kind of want to impress."

She thought for a second.

Then she said, "Tell me her locker number."

When she stepped off the train, Bates and Crash shot immediately over to where I was sitting. They started gushing, flooding me with questions and exclamations. I tried my best to answer, but I was totally gone — staring out the window at the night, shivering, lost in the wonder of my own gloriously weird life.

We got the letter in the mail a few days later, delivered by certified post. We'd never gotten one of those before. It was a Saturday morning. At first, I think, I didn't even really believe it was true. I mean, did special deliveries even *happen* on Saturdays? But the doorbell rang and my mom walked over to the big grated garage door and grabbed the latch and swung it open.

The letter carrier looked around our suddenly exposed kitchen, confused as anything.

"I need to have somebody sign for this," he told my mother. "Registered mail. It's addressed to the Glazer family, North Diamond Street at this address?"

"That's us," my mom said, plucking the letter from his fingers.

Ignoring him, she ran to the kitchen table, grabbed a butcher knife, and sliced it open. Hastily, apologetically, my father scribbled his name across the clipboard.

I leaped up from my stool. The spoon clattered on the edge of my cereal bowl indecisively, wavered for a moment, and finally plunged the wrong way down onto the unfinished surface of the kitchen counter. I felt nervous, but I was afraid to even feel that. It was probably nothing. A letter from our family in Zvrackova, a request for a parent-teacher on the subject of my increasingly lousy grades.

My mother held it up to the light and started to read.

Her face went through a series of emotions. Confusion, impassivity, meditative pleased-ness. "Is us!" she cried, finally, triumphantly. "Is *ours*!"

"What's ours?" I exclaimed, although the sensation in my chest was a curious buzz, as though my lungs and nerves had thrown themselves a preemptory victory party and were well on their way to getting drunk. I hesitated to think that I already knew the answer.

"The factory!" she cried. "The letter is from Goldberg, says that company has found another factory to sell! Our company is going to buy — we don't got to move!"

She ran to my father, flung herself with arms wide, small trails of fat wobbling near her elbows, and squeezed his scant chest tight. He adjusted his glasses. From behind, a single solitary tear gleamed, and in the space of a second — before he waved at me with a still-hugging arm, calling me over to join in the family celebration — I thought it was a diamond, rolling down his cheek.

The next morning in the special schoolwide assembly where a 9/11 survivor recounted his tale of horror and lectured us about how to be upstanding citizens, Devin Murray walked right up to the front row where I was sitting and planted a big, loud, and not totally embarrassing kiss on my cheek. Her lips lingered there for several seconds. It wasn't at all like the hard, quick kiss that my mother gave me on the forehead every night before bed. Devin's was soft, gentle, sensual, and gummy — almost like, in those few seconds and those few centimeters, her entire body had glided against that small square of cheek, stimulating me almost to the point of physical materialization. I shot down fast into the fold-able wooden seat, hoping that none of the 690 freshmen in the rows behind me would notice my manifesting arousal. Luckily, they were too busy hooting me on to pay it any heed.

I mean, I didn't even know what my reward was for.

It wasn't until that night, sitting on the roof of the factory — *our* factory — that Vadim told me how a 150-gallon beer keg had spontaneously materialized in the second-floor corridor, directly in front of Devin's locker, when school had opened that morning. And it had sat there, uninterrupted — although several teachers and Dr. Mayhew demanded to know how it had gotten there, what it was doing, but since it was empty, there was no point trying to suspend anyone — until the middle of second period, when Devin phoned the deposit place and had two men in brown delivery uniforms pick it up.

"And that, my friend," Vadim finished with a flourish, "is how cool you really are. You solve up the whole case, and you don't even have to be there to do it."

"Thanks," I said, surprised by the sudden weariness in my own voice. "But I don't really feel like being cool anymore."

I said it, thinking that it was just a basic statement of fact, like not being hungry anymore at the end of dinner, or not feeling like playing baseball anymore, now that summer's over. But it felt right. Ever since I moved to America, I had teachers and parents and guidance counselors telling me, *You'll find your place.* At first, I thought that it was something you had to win, like first place. As if once I scored an A on five straight tests, then I'd get to hang out with Reg or Devin as a reward.

Now that I had — not that I'd scored any As on tests, but now that I'd hung out with both of them — it didn't feel like such a thrill. The whole idea of *finding your place* seemed to make more sense, at least in my head, but I still hadn't settled on any one place yet. Hanging out with Crash and Bates seemed fun. It wasn't what I wanted to do with the rest of my life. Hell, it wasn't even what I wanted to do with the rest of my week. But it was cool to know that, whenever I wanted to hang out with them, they were there to be hung out with. I could pretty much go on whatever path I wanted, end up in whatever place I wanted to be in. Even Margie probably was hang-outable — and she wouldn't be that hard to find.

But, for now, here was where I wanted to be. In my own little world, and on top of it. We were well into September by now, and the sunsets were definitely getting earlier. Beneath Vadim and me, the Yards twinkled like the inverted sky of an alternate universe, dull yellow streetlights and fluorescent white factory lights glowing instead of stars. The minty green glow of Vadim's laptop illuminated our faces as we gazed out into the universe below us.

"Dude," Vadim said, "I bet I could hack into your family's factory software and get all the machines to form little steel *J*s if you wanted."

"Nah." I shook my head. "Cool idea, but we'd have to reprogram everything before work tomorrow."

"'We'? Does this mean you're rejoining the corporate workforce?"

I offered up a wry grin. "Maybe," I admitted. "For now, anyway. I figure, if I want my life to continue in the manner to which I have become accustomed, I'd better start making some money to keep it that way."

Vadim mulled that one over. "Good idea," he announced, finally. "Hey, you think I could get hired by the CIA? As a computer person or something?"

I shrugged. "If you want it hard enough, you could do anything you want."

"Cool," Vadim agreed absently. He turned back to his computer, hit a few keys, then passed through screens silently. After a few minutes, the reflection of the screen on his face lit up, changing from pale green to a vivid, liquid red, and so did his eyes. "Hey," he said, the lowercase *o* of his mouth widening. "Nessa Greyscole's having a party tonight over at a warehouse on Delaware Ave. You want to crash it with me?"

By the time it occurred to me to answer, the streets had turned a deep, dark, cat's-eye shade of gray, and the activity was dim, limited to a few old men playing chess under the streetlight, the wino down the street tapping out an old jazz song on his empty malt liquor bottle.

"No, thanks. I might catch up later," I told him, knowing full well that I didn't intend to catch up at all. "But you should go."

"Really? You think so?"

I had a momentary thought, the briefest flutter of an idea — that I should tell him what I *really* thought of it — but the notion passed, and it was too late. He was already throwing one foot over the wall, scampering all the way down to the street.

Curiously, though, I didn't mind. I wasn't offended at all, as a matter of fact.

I lay down, threw my arms over the steel pipe, and stared up at the stars.

THANK YOUSE

So this story started at Central High in Philly, the geek school, the school that kind of saved my life. Thanks to my Northeast crew, for getting me out of there, and to the downtown and Mt. Airy kids, for giving me somewhere to land.

This book, though, started off right after I got engaged, and Itta had to get back to Australia, and we got to the airport two hours early because I am paranoid. She went to sleep on the bench and I started writing. So this book is kind of hers — for putting up with my geekiness and not letting it outshine her own, and for sharing our nuptials with my iBook.

Yalta, my bouncing ball of light. My next of kin. For sitting tight for nine months and listening to me read my book out loud and sing Ani Difranco songs to you.

Mom, Mum, Tuddy, and Dad. Grandmom. Alyssa. Cuz. Brothers, sisters, and all the outlaw in-laws from Oz.

Dr. Pavel, Ms. Schroeder, Mr. Zeff, and all the MG teachers who kept me on the right side of trouble. Zack and Liz. Berwin, the most eligible bachelor in Melbourne. DJ Odin Smith (www.myspace.com/odinsmithlabs). Fred Chao & Johnny Thro (half Asian, all hero). Mat (www.wanderjew.com). Prowler (www.myspace.com/prowler1). CJ and my band, Chibi Vision (www.myspace.com/chibivision).

Grandpop, and the War of 1066.

Cristin, Kim, Adams & the O'Donnell family, Michelle, Eric, Shmop. Ludacris, Tori, and The Cure.

The team at HQ. Erin, Ranya, Jody, and the notorious S.M.E. The original Joshua Gee. And David: You are my Mr. Patterson, and you can rescue me from evil thugs any day of the week. And you do.

Luke, Richard Nash & Anne Horowitz at Soft Skull. Big tovaritschsky love to Jake, Ellen, Kas, Uncle Chaim, and all the hidden Russian tzaddikim out there.

This book is for Mike, who was right with me on every step of the journey, from getting beat up together in the Northeast to sneaking into Central (sorry, Dr. Pavel). You taught me how to dress, how to dance, and you let me let my nerd light shine. No fair, ducking out before our big finale.

Fixed
2-13-12